"Sharp, funny and playful...Homes is confident and consistent in her odd departures from life as we know it, sustaining credibility by getting details right. A fully engaged imagination [is] at work—and at play."

—Amy Hempel,
Los Angeles Times Book Review

"A. M. Homes' provocative and funny and sometimes very sad takes on contemporary suburban life impressed me enormously. The more bizarre things get, the more impressed one is by A. M. Homes' skills as a realist, a portraitist of contemporary life at its most perverse."

—David Leavitt

"A. M. Homes finds mystery without special effects or exotic under-bellies. We get a tour through the action adventure of everyday fantasies. Many of Homes' characters lead two lives, one on God's most conventional little acre, one in some alternate universe."

—*Mirabella*

"An unnerving glimpse through the windows of other people's lives. A. M. Homes is a provocative and eloquent writer, and her vision of the way we live now is anything but safe."

—Meg Wolitzer

"Set in a world filled with edges to topple from, [*The Safety of Objects*] is permeated by the bizarre....The unexpected emerges from the story itself, startling and unexpectedly right."

—*Cleveland Plain Dealer*

"A. M. Homes has a real gift for using a single, sharp tool to make (or suggest, perhaps) an astute general observation. With little she makes much, a trait I much admire in these days of profuse and prolix novels."

—Doris Grumbach

"Homes' surprises proceed out of a stranger, surrealistic fictional world ...One way or another, there's no place like Homes and her stories."

—*San Francisco Examiner*

THE SAFETY
OF OBJECTS

Also by A. M. Homes

JACK

THE SAFETY OF OBJECTS

STORIES BY

A. M. HOMES

VINTAGE CONTEMPORARIES

Vintage Books · A Division of Random House, Inc. · New York

First Vintage Contemporaries Edition, November 1991

Acknowledgment is made to the periodicals in which some of
these stories originally appeared:

"Looking for Johnny," "The I of It," and "A Real Doll" in
Christopher Street; "Yours Truly" and "Esther in the Night"
in *Story;* "Chunky in Heat" in *Between C&D;* "Slumber
Party" in *New York Woman.*

Library of Congress Cataloging-in-Publication Data
Homes, A. M.
    The safety of objects : stories / by A. M. Homes.—1st
  Vintage contemporaries ed.
      p. cm.—(Vintage contemporaries)
    Originally published: New York : Norton, 1990.
    ISBN 0-679-73629-8 (pbk.)
    I. Title.
[PS3558.0448S2 1991]
813'.54—dc20   91-50019
                CIP

Manufactured in the United States of America

10 9 8 7 6 5 4 3 2 1

The author wishes to thank Randall Kenan,
Neil B. Olson, The Corporation of Yaddo, and
the Department of English/Creative Writing
at New York University for their support.

To Eric and Alice

CONTENTS

THE SAFETY
OF OBJECTS

ADULTS ALONE

Elaine takes the boys to Florida and drops them off like they're dry cleaning.

"See you in ten days," she says as they wave good-bye in the American terminal. "Be nice!"

She kisses her mother-in-law's cheek and, feeling the rough skin against her own, thinks of this woman literally as her husband's genetic map, down to the beard.

"Go," her mother-in-law says, pushing her towards the gate.

It is the first time she's left her children like that. She gets back onto the plane thinking there's something wrong with her, that she should have a better reason or a better vacation plan, Europe not Westchester.

Paul is waiting at the airport. He's been there all day. After dropping them off this morning, he took over the west end of the lounge and spent the day there working. She knows because he paged her at Miami International to remind her to bring oranges home.

He seems younger than she remembers. His eyes are glowing and he looks a little bit like Charlie Manson did before he let himself go. Elaine is sure he's been smoking dope again. She imagines Paul locking himself in an airport bathroom stall with his smokeless pipe and some guy who got bumped off a flight to L.A.

She wonders why he doesn't find it strange, pressing himself into a tiny metal cabinet with a total stranger. He once told her that whenever he got stoned in a bathroom with another guy it gave him a hard-on and he was never sure if it was the dope or the other man.

She can't believe that in all these years he's never been busted. She used to wish it would happen; she thought it would straighten him out.

"Let's go home," Elaine says.

"We don't have to go home, we can go anywhere. We can. . . ." He winks at her.

"I'm tired," Elaine says.

They drive home silently. The car is so new that it doesn't make any noises. Paul pulls carefully into the driveway. Branches from trees surrounding the house scrape across the car. Elaine thinks of campfire horror stories about men with hooks for arms and women buried alive with long fingernails poking through the dirt.

"Got to cut those branches back," Paul says and then they are silent.

Paul follows her up the steps, talking about the steps. "If we're going to paint them, we should go ahead and do it before it snows."

"Maybe tomorrow," she says, but honestly she doesn't want to do anything else to the house. She's given up on it. It's too much work.

She feels like she's been having an extramarital relationship with their home. It isn't even an affair, an affair sounds too nice, too good. As far as she's concerned a house should be like a self-cleaning oven; it should take care of itself.

The last time she was happy with the house was the day before they moved in, when the floors had just been done, when it was big and empty, and they hadn't paid for it yet.

Elaine pushes open the front door.

"I wish you'd remember to lock the door," she says. "In the city you never forgot to lock the door."

It is dark inside. Elaine stands in the front hall, trying to remember where the light switch is. In the six months they've lived there, she and Paul have never been alone in the house. It's nice, she thinks, still feeling the wall for the switch. She turns on all the lights and begins picking up things, Daniel's clothing, Sammy's toys. She straightens the pillows on the sofa and goes upstairs to take a bath. The phone rings and Paul answers it. She falls asleep hearing the sound of voices softly talking, thinking Paul is a good father; he is down the hall, reading a story to Sammy.

As usual they both wake between six-thirty and seven, listening for the children. They are alone together, trapped in their bed. They don't have to get up. They don't have to go anywhere. They are on vacation.

Eventually, between seven-thirty and quarter-to-eight, when there is no more getting around it, she looks at him. He is balding. She thinks she can actually see his hairline receding, follicle by follicle. He has told her that he can feel it. He says his whole head feels different; it tingles, it gets chilled easily, it just isn't the way it used to be. She thinks about herself. Her face is caving in. She has circles and bags and all kinds of things around her eyes. Last week she spent forty dollars on lotion to cover it all up.

When she comes downstairs, he has already eaten breakfast and lunch.

"Maybe we should go to a movie later?" he says.

Paul doesn't really mean they should go to a movie; he means they should make a time to be together, in some way or another. Usually they have to get a sitter for this.

"Pick you up around four," he says.

"Does that mean you're taking the car? I have things to do."

"We can go together," he says.

In his fantasy about suburban life the whole family is always in the car together, going places, singing songs, eating McDonald's. He loves it when they pull up in front of a store and he goes in while she waits in the car for as long as it takes.

"Forget it," she says.

Late in the afternoon, Paul comes into the bedroom where Elaine is resting.

"I brought you something," he says, handing her a porno tape he rented in town.

"For me?" she says.

She can't imagine that he brought this for her. If he was going to bring her a present she'd like flowers, a scarf, even a record. Porno is not a gift.

He puts the tape in the VCR. They are so used to each other that it doesn't take long, and after a short nap they decide to actually go to the movies.

The marquee isn't lit and Elaine has to put on Paul's glasses in order to see what's playing. He says something about smoking a joint in the theater, but she reminds him that they both have professional reputations.

"You never know where your clients might be," she says. "Besides," she whispers in his ear, "this isn't Manhattan."

She puts her hand on his crotch and squeezes. She knows he likes it when she does things like that in public places.

In the darkness of the theater they fall in love. They fall in love not so much with each other, that's history, but in love with the idea of being in love, of liking someone that much. She puts her head on his shoulder and he doesn't say anything about it hurting his tennis arm.

After the movie, they walk down the main street. Paul walks with his hands in his pockets and Elaine keeps her arms wrapped tightly around her chest like she's protecting herself from something. It's as if in the dark theater they swore they'd be in love for the entire week, but outside in the fresh air, neither is sure it's viable.

Elaine and Paul cut across the street and go into the only restaurant in town where they can both eat without getting sick. Paul orders a bottle of wine. He orders fettuccine alfredo without checking with Elaine. She doesn't say anything about his cholesterol. It's part of their love agreement. They are for the moment Siamese twins separated. They are off-duty parole officers. They are free. Their sons are in Florida being overfed by his mother.

In the car on the way home they smoke two joints. She tells Paul to drive by the sound before going back to the house. He parks at the edge of the water, turns off the engine, and they sit looking out, across to whatever it is that's out there, maybe Connecticut.

"Did you think we'd ever be here, like this?" Elaine asks.

"Here like what?"

"Here, in a house, with a station wagon?"

A light flashes across their car, and instead of going on it freezes on Elaine and Paul. There is a knock on Paul's window and the flashlight shines in.

"Roll down your window, sir?" the police officer says. "Can I help you? Are you looking for something?"

"Just taking in the view," Paul says.

Elaine thinks they're being busted, the cop smells the dope. She can't believe she's in the car and this is happening, now, to her. She hardly ever gets stoned.

Even though it's early October, Paul is beginning to

sweat. Elaine thinks he'll turn them in. He's reminding her of Dagwood Bumstead.

"We just moved here six months ago," Elaine says.

It's always her job to take care of things. To deal. If they are arrested, they will have to move, immediately, before the boys come home. There will be a picture of her on the front page of the local paper. NEWCOMER UP IN SMOKE.

"Do you have any identification? May I see your license, sir?"

The cop looks like he's twelve years old. If he ever shaves it's not because he has to, but because it makes him feel older.

"Is this your current address?"

"No, we live here at three-four-three-three Maplerock Terrace," Elaine says.

She smiles at the cop. He doesn't ask for her license. She's the wife.

The cop's whole head is inside the car, but he doesn't seem to smell anything. Elaine decides that either he's retarded or has a serious sinus problem.

"You're new here," he says.

"That's right. I'm even a member of the newcomers club, meets once a month," Elaine says, determined to keep them out of jail.

"Well," the cop says. "Why don't you go on home now."

"We were just taking in the view," Paul says, nodding towards the sound.

"We don't do that here, sir," the cop says. "Have a good evening, sir," the cop says.

He turns off his flashlight and walks back to the squad car.

Paul doesn't start the car right away. He doesn't seem able to. He's covered with a slimy film of sweat. His skin is glow-in-the-dark white.

"Are you in pain?" Elaine asks.

She turns on the map light so she can get a better look at him.

"Are you having a heart attack?"

She wishes she hadn't let him order the fettuccine.

"Should I take you to the hospital?"

"Drive home?" he says.

She opens her door and goes around to the other side. The cop is parked down the block, lights off, watching them.

Paul crosses over inside the car. His legs get stuck on the gear shift and it is a few minutes before Elaine can get in. She stands in the street, waiting. She thinks about what would happen in an emergency, if Paul really had to stand up to something, a burglar maybe.

During the night Paul's stomach starts in and toxic clouds billow silently from his sleeping body. Elaine goes into Sammy's room and buries herself among the stuffed animals, using the big bear for a pillow and a husband.

At around seven Paul wakes Elaine by trying to fit himself next to her in the twin bed.

"You smelled terrible," she says.

"Why did you let me have the fettuccine?"

She doesn't say anything. It's too complicated. She let him eat it because she doesn't like him and doesn't care what he does and wishes he would die soon. She let him eat it because she loves him and can't deny him his pleasures and is determined not to act like his mother.

He starts to make love to her.

"Not here," she says, thinking it's an incredibly perverted thing to do in their child's bed.

He stops and curls next to her. She rolls in towards the wall, pulling the Mickey Mouse blanket up over her head. Without the children, with nothing absolutely required of her, she is exhausted. She is more tired than she ever remembers being.

She dreams that her children have been attacked by a shark. She hears her mother-in-law telling her the story, long distance.

"They're fine, that's the most important thing. In the history of Miami Beach, it never happened before. Sammy was lying at the edge of the water, not really even in the water, and a shark, a very small shark, washed up on top of him. And Daniel, what a big boy, what a man, reached down and pulled the shark off Sammy, but then the shark got Daniel by the arm. It wasn't a big shark. It must have been dying because why else was it on the beach? Daniel just shook it off. No skin broken. It's here now, in the bathtub. The boys want to have it stuffed. I said it's up to you. You're the mother."

At noon Elaine gets out of bed, and pulls on the same clothing she wore yesterday. She doesn't bother to brush her teeth. She isn't going to run into anyone she has to talk to. Elaine takes the car to the grocery store. She sits in the parking lot staring at the store. She hates it, but figures that since she's already there, she'll be a good sport, she'll run in.

Elaine picks out items that are strictly for adults only, foods her children would never let her buy: smelly cheese, paté, crackers with seeds, wine. It adds up to thirty-nine dollars and somehow fits into one bag.

"My mother called," Paul says as she walks into the house.

He is on a ladder in the hallway, changing a bulb that burned out three months ago.

"Is everything all right?" she asks, thinking of the shark dream.

"Sammy misses you. They'll call back."

She crosses under the ladder and goes into the kitchen.

"Bad luck, under the ladder," he says.

She makes herself a huge plate of food, takes a bottle of wine, and crosses back under the ladder on her way upstairs.

"Are you planning to share?"

She doesn't answer him. She knows he can't imagine her eating all that. She hates food, and yet she is hungry; she is so hungry that she can't wait to get upstairs where she can be alone with the food, where she can dig in without an audience.

"I'm changing the bulb, didn't you notice?"

She knows she's supposed to think he's wonderful for finally doing something. But as far as she's concerned, he's wasting time. Elaine throws a grape at him. It hits his chest and falls into his shirt.

"Grapes cost three dollars a pound," he says. "I thought we agreed not to buy them. The boys just squish them between their fingers and leave them on the table."

"The boys are away," she says, and continues up the stairs.

She sits in the middle of their bed with her plate. Something is missing: olives, onions, garnishes. She carries the plate back downstairs.

Paul is sitting in the chair in front of the TV, in broad daylight, with a glass of Hawaiian Punch in his hand. He looks like a demented version of the suburban man, the Playboy man, the man in his castle.

She takes a sip from his glass. It is tainted. There is something wrong with the punch. She thinks about supermarket tampering, murder in the suburbs, and how much she hates food. She thinks she's going to die.

"There's something wrong with the punch," she says, coughing.

"There's vodka in it," he says, taking the glass back from her.

She takes her plate and goes into the kitchen, planning to pile it higher, then go back upstairs and never come down. She stands inside the refrigerator door, snacking. She hates eating in the kitchen. It makes her think about cleaning up and then she loses her appetite.

She carries her plate into the living room.

Paul is on the floor two feet from the TV, sitting cross-legged, his drink in his crotch, playing with Daniel's Nintendo. There's a driving game on the screen. He crashes again and again. Paul's been driving for more than twenty years. He should be able to get through a game; she's seen Daniel do it a million times.

In a way it's cute, Paul playing like a little boy, falling into the TV. But there's also something incredibly pathetic about it.

"Could you turn it down a little?" Elaine asks.

Paul's car slips off the road and crashes into a billboard. The car bursts into flames and *Game Over, Game Over* flashes across the screen.

"Can't you see I'm doing something?" he screams, pushing the restart button.

"You're playing a game."

"Leave me alone."

Elaine goes back upstairs. She can't stand him. She can't stand anything about him: the way he thinks, talks, looks, all of it. She knows he hates her too and that makes it even worse. It makes her nuts. She should be able to hate him without any backlash.

She sits in the middle of their bed with her plate and turns on the TV. She sits in front of it, staring at it, and then gets upset when she realizes that she's been watching golf for at least a half hour.

She pours herself a glass of wine, puts a piece of cheese

on a cracker, and leans back on her pillow. She drinks the wine and then pours herself another glass. It's so nice, she thinks, to lie in your bed and drink and not worry about drinking too much, about having to be on duty, like a nurse in a ward, so fucking responsible.

She feels like she's floating. She feels wonderful. She wishes she could do this every day. It would make her life so much better. The phone rings and she ignores it. It rings and rings, and finally she has to pick it up.

"Mommy," Sammy's small voice says. "Mommy, why did you leave me here?"

She sits up in bed, spilling the glass of wine all over her shirt.

"I didn't leave you there, sweetie, I brought you there to be with Grandma, to go to the beach, to swim. You're on vacation, honey."

She can't believe how drunk she is; she's trying to be normal, to sound like herself.

"I don't want to be on vacation," he says.

There's a silence and then nothing. She wonders if her child has hung up on her. She wonders what kind of a mother she is.

"He'll be fine," her mother-in-law says. Her voice is deep from smoking and she sounds like Milton Berle. "I gave him some chocolate milk and cookies. I told him he has his brother and me. We'll see how it goes."

"If he's not hungry don't make him eat," Elaine says.

She doesn't want her child growing up with an eating disorder. She doesn't want him fat or thin. She wants him just right.

"Make him eat? How could I make him eat? I put it on the plate. If he wants it, he eats it, my little prince. And Daniel, I think he's starting to like girls. All around the pool, they crowd around him. Hold on, I'll get him that misses his mother so much."

Elaine is nauseated. Her mother-in-law is too much, too strong. She waits on the world hand and foot. Compared to her, Elaine is nothing.

"Mommy," Sammy says, "why did you bring me here and leave me?"

"I just told you, baby, you're on vacation."

"When are you coming to take me home?"

"Grandma is bringing you home next week. You'll be tan and beautiful."

"I want to come home now. Come and get me now."

"I can't do that, sweetie. I'm here with Daddy. Have a good time with Grandma and I'll see you soon."

He starts to cry. She is annoyed. She's annoyed, and then she can't believe how selfish she's being. This is her child, her baby. How could she be angry? How could she have gone to the grocery store and not bought anything for him, no animal crackers, Ho-Ho's, nothing he likes?

"Oh, baby, it's all right. I miss you too, you're my boy, I'll call you again later. Tell Grandma to give you another cookie."

In the background Sammy is crying and Daniel is laughing. Mixed messages. She hangs up the phone, takes off her wine-soaked shirt, and tries to remember what you do to get wine stains out. She drops the shirt onto the floor, lies back on the bed in her bra, and pours herself another glass of wine.

Paul comes upstairs and asks what's for dinner. She hands him a cracker with cheese. He lies down next to her on the bed.

"Did you take a shower today?" she asks.

He looks insulted. "I've been working all day."

"You didn't take a shower. You smell."

He kisses her.

"Your face hurts," she says. "I can't kiss you when you don't shave."

In the old days when they were on vacation, they would shower together, make love, and then change into good clothes and go out for dinner. Now Elaine is lying half-naked on a crumb-covered bed, smelling like cheap rosé. Paul pulls off his shirt and sticks his nose into his armpit. "It's not so bad," he says.

"You must have a blockage in your nose. Maybe you should see an ear, nose, and throat man."

He lies down next to her. She picks up the platter from the floor and puts it between them. They eat and pass the wine glass back and forth. When the plate is empty and the bed scratchy with cracker crumbs, they roll over and fall asleep.

In his sleep Paul knocks the empty glass off the bed and onto the floor. The stem snaps off.

At ten o'clock Paul gets out of bed and steps on the glass. Elaine spends the next half hour pulling pieces of glass out of Paul's foot. She presses gauze pads soaked in peroxide against his wounds, and he yells into her ear. She feels like Florence Nightingale.

There is blood on the sheets, and on the floor. Little pieces of broken glass are everywhere.

Her wine-stained shirt is still on the floor. The empty plate is on the floor. They pull off the rest of their clothing, and curl up next to each other for warmth.

The television is still on, but they can't find the remote control. They end up watching a special half-hour report on crack.

As they're watching it, they're both thinking it looks great. It looks fun.

When the report is over, they are quiet for a minute, uncomfortable, and then he turns to her and says, "I think I can get some?"

"When?" she asks.

"Tomorrow," he says.

She turns away from him, puts her head down on the pillow, and falls asleep, looking forward, for the first time in a long time, to tomorrow.

"When are you getting the crack?" she asks, as soon as she wakes up.

"I'll make some calls," he says.

"This morning?" she asks.

"It's going to take hours just to find someone who knows a crack dealer," he says.

Elaine tells Paul she has errands to run. She gets in the car and spends two and a half hours driving around—practically in circles because she doesn't want to go too far, she doesn't want to get lost.

By the time she gets home the crack is there. Somehow Paul found a dealer who delivers.

It has been forever since either of them did anything new. Buying the house, moving out there was new, but it was also something they were expected to do. It was destiny.

There are six vials on the dining room table.

"Is that a lot or a little?" she asks.

Paul shrugs. "I dunno," he says. "It's too new for me." He pauses. "Remember me?" he says. "Remember when I was young and had hair and knew about things?"

She nods. She remembers him twelve years ago, when he was young and brilliant and there was no one else like him.

"At least you knew where to get it," she says.

"We may not like it," he says.

"I like it already," Elaine says.

Paul puts the crack into a pipe he also bought from the dealer and Elaine begins to get nervous. It is too exciting. She can't believe they are actually going to do this. It's so not like them, not the way anyone would expect them to be.

Paul lights the pipe and draws in. The dining room fills with a smell that is at the same time familiar and completely unfamiliar, something vaguely like a doctor's office or the house late on Thursday afternoon just after the maid's gone home. She is not sure if it is the crack burning or the pipe melting. Paul scrunches his eyes closed, tilts his head back, and hands the pipe to her. She puts a little more of the crack rock in and nervously lights it.

Elaine has the sensation of being a fountain. She herself is the fountain in front of the Plaza Hotel. Sparks pour out of her and bounce across the ground before dying out. She is a Roman candle. It is so good that she almost can't stand it. She has to sit down. She has to lie down on the living room sofa. She has to smoke again as soon as the sensation starts to fade.

"This is your brain. This is your brain on drugs." An image of a fried egg on television. A commercial. Sammy had looked at the TV and said, "No it's not, that's my breakfast," and then collapsed laughing onto the floor.

Between then and midnight they go through four vials. When they stop it is only because they have the sensation that their bodies can't stand anymore. They are sweating profusely. Paul starts taking his pulse every five minutes and writing it down.

"I'm making a graph," he says. "Let me take yours too. Me in blue, you in red."

Elaine doesn't answer him. She goes into the kitchen, opens the freezer, and digs out a spoonful of ice cream. It feels like velvet in her throat.

"What are you doing?" Paul yells from the living room.

"Nothing," she says.

She smells the crack burning again.

"My pulse is a hundred and eighty," Paul says.

"Isn't that aerobic?" Elaine yells in to him. She is pleased that she can be witty and stoned all at once.

Suddenly, in the kitchen, she gets nervous that someone will call, the parent of one of her children's friends, someone in a carpool, and on the phone she'll say something that will ruin her life or at least her future. She turns on the answering machine.

Paul screams from the living room. He doesn't say anything, he just screams as loud as he can. Elaine runs in and tells him to stop.

"You have ice cream on your face," Paul says, and then starts screaming again.

"You're upsetting me," she says. "I felt so good before, and now I feel as if everything is strange, everything is ruined."

Paul stops screaming and holds his wife. He holds her and hands her the pipe. "Just do a little more," he says. "And then we'll stop. Just get it good again."

And so she does one more, and it is good again, and the living room looks so nice and their halogen lights are so bright and modern. They are alone together in their house.

They lie on the sofa, having silent conversations with each other. The voices in their heads are so loud that neither realizes that they aren't actually talking.

Finally, at about three in the morning, they begin to unwind, the lights seem too bright, and Paul gets up and turns them off, then picks up the two leftover vials and puts them in his pocket.

They go upstairs to bed, but neither sleeps. They turn the television off and on and fight about who should have control of the remote and how often they should change channels. At five in the morning, Elaine gets out of bed and brings them each a Valium. It's like a party favor.

They pop them into their mouths and swallow without water.

Elaine wakes up, dying of thirst and craving sugar. She can't remember if they ate dinner last night. Walking down the steps she feels uncoordinated, spastic, as though she has a neurological disease. She feels the age of her body and the weight of gravity. Everything pulls towards the ground.

Elaine stands naked in the kitchen, sucking the last drops of Berry Red from a cardboard box of Hawaiian Punch. She shifts the straw around and for a second it slips out of her mouth. A little bit of the bright red drink rolls down her neck.

The doorbell rings and then rings again. She freezes. She thinks it's the police. The neighbors smelled the crack burning.

Elaine is naked in the kitchen, there is no way out, no way to get anywhere without passing windows. There is only a dishtowel too small to cover anything.

There is a knock at the door and a man calls her name. "Misses?" She crouches down so that if he comes around the side of the house, he can't see her. Elaine slides across the floor and checks the calendar. It is written in that someone is coming to measure for carpet. She creeps over to the door, reaching up to check that it is locked. He knocks on the front door again.

"Anybody home?"

She is afraid he will try the knob and it will open. The carpet man will find her on the floor naked. Everyone knows that in a house you're supposed to wear a bathrobe. People will talk about it. They'll say she's an alcoholic, she must have passed out like that. They'll ask each other if she walks around naked when the children are home. They'll stop letting their kids sleep over.

On her stomach she crawls across the linoleum towards the coat closet in the hall. When she gets there she opens the door and stands up inside the closet. Her stomach and breasts are covered with lint and dirt. She puts on Paul's black cashmere overcoat and opens the door.

The police officer is there. It is the same police officer from the other night.

Elaine wonders if you can bust someone retroactively.

"Is there a problem?" Elaine asks.

"Somehow, I didn't give your husband back his license. It took me a while to find you. The old address and all," he says.

She takes the license from the cop. "Thank you."

The cop nods. "No problem."

She wonders if he knows that she's naked inside the coat. She wonders what he thinks of that. The phone rings.

"Telephone, ma'am," the cop says.

"Oh, right, thanks again," Elaine says.

"I'm bringing the boys home early," her mother-in-law says. Her voice is amplified by the answering machine. It sounds like God is talking.

Elaine turns off the machine and picks up the phone. "Is something wrong?"

"The baby is too young to be without his mother."

She doesn't understand what is going on. She wonders if maybe her mother-in-law is slipping, getting too old to deal with children.

"Daniel came to me early, but that was different," her mother-in-law says. "You put him in day care at eight months. He didn't know you. He didn't need you."

"What does that mean?"

"Nothing, just that Sammy is different; it's always that

way with the youngest." Her mother-in-law doesn't say anything for a minute. "The plane gets in at five."

Mother is coming, Mother is here, everything is going to be all right, Elaine thinks.

Elaine goes upstairs, wakes Paul and tells him. They are both silent. They are protective of their freedom. There are other things they want to do. They want to go further. They want to be alone with each other, and alone with themselves.

Paul and Elaine stand in the center of their bedroom, undressing. Paul pulls the bandage from his foot, and strips off his underwear. Elaine strips the sheets off the bed, goes down the hall, strips the sheets in her sons' room, and stuffs everything into the laundry chute. They smile at each other. They shower together. In the shower, Paul shaves and Elaine scrubs the tiles with the fingernail brush, not getting out until the whole wall is done.

Elaine combs her wet hair back and Paul tells her she looks beautiful.

"It was good," Elaine says.

Paul puts clean Band-Aids on his foot. They dress. In a way they are relieved. Together they put clean sheets on the beds, puff the pillows, vacuum the bedroom, empty the trash, and load the dishwasher. Downstairs as they are cleaning, Elaine and Paul look at each other and as if they've each had the same thought at the same moment, as if they're sharing a secret, they go into the living room and carefully check the cushions on the sofa making sure there's nothing there, no empty vials.

LOOKING FOR JOHNNY

I disappeared a few years ago; I disappeared and then I came back. It wasn't a big secret. It wasn't one of those beam-me-up-Scotty deals where I was here and then all of the sudden I was there. I didn't get to go to another planet or anything. I was gone for a few days and then I came home and the police wanted to know everything. They wanted to know about the car, who was in the car, where I went, what happened. They said I could draw pictures, show them with dolls, but I didn't know what to say. I disappeared when I was a child. I disappeared when I was nine.

I came home from school, had cookies and Kool-Aid, and went into the living room to watch TV. My retarded sister Rayanne was in there and she kept imitating the people on TV. She was older than me and really was retarded. She kept talking to the television and didn't stop when I told her to. Finally, I couldn't stand it anymore so I left. I said, " 'Bye, Mom, be back in a while," and I picked up my basketball and went to the playground. There were other kids there and almost everyone had their own ball. There were about ten balls going and sometimes they would hit each other in mid-air and go off in completely the wrong direction. Sometimes I'd trip over another guy going in for a shot and he might kick me in the butt and say "Asshole," or something.

It got late and it got dark and the other kids left one by one or sometimes in twos and threes. I was alone on the court shooting baskets, and I couldn't miss. The ball kept dropping through the net and I felt like I had magic in me. I was making all my shots, counting them to myself. When I got to fifteen in a row, I heard someone clap. I stopped playing and noticed a guy standing at the far edge of the court.

"That's fifteen straight up," he said. I shrugged. I shot again and the ball sailed through the hoop.

"Nice going, Johnny."

I caught the ball coming through the hoop and put up a hook shot. It went wide. The guy ran in, caught the ball, and held it pressed into his hip, like a teacher confiscating it.

"My name's not Johnny."

"Johnny's not a name. It's like 'hey you,' only nicer."

He bounced the ball a couple of times and then held it. "You ready to go? Your mother said I should pick you up. She had somewhere to go."

I remember being mad at my mother because she was like that. She was the kind of person who would take Rayanne somewhere and send someone I didn't know to pick me up. She knew lots of people I didn't know, mostly on account of Rayanne. She knew all the people who had retarded kids and I never wanted to meet them.

"I was looking for you, Johnny," the guy said.

I shrugged. "My name's Erol. Okay? Erol," I said.

He kept my basketball and walked towards his car. It was an old white station wagon, a Rambler with a red interior.

"Did she have to take my sister somewhere?"

"It's okay, Johnny. We'll stop at McDonald's."

He talked like he didn't hear anything I said. He talked like it was something he had to practice in order to get it right.

"Are you hungry?"

I'm not retarded. If something had been really strange, like if the guy had a wooden leg, I would have noticed. I would have gotten up from the table and walked away. I would have walked when he got up and said he was going to call my mom. He said he was calling to ask if she wanted us to bring home food for them. He left me at the table with burgers and fries and I thought more about how many of his fries I could steal than whether or not I was ever going home again. I had no reason to leave; I was at McDonald's with two burgers, large fries, and a shake. I didn't know what crazy was. I didn't know that sometimes you can't tell the difference between a real crazy and a regular person and that's what makes them crazy in the first place.

The guy came back, said my mother wasn't home, and that he was going to take me to his house until she got back. "Hey, hey, Johnny," the guy said. In the car I played with my basketball. I turned it around and around on my lap.

"I have to pick up something. Is that okay, Johnny? Do you want anything?" I shook my head. "Is there anything you want?"

"No," I said.

I waited while he went into the drugstore. It was one of those times when the sun goes down but it isn't dark yet. There was a weird blue light pressing down on everything, outlining it. I stood next to the station wagon and bounced the basketball.

"Hello, Erol," Mrs. Perkins said. She was pushing a grocery cart across the parking lot even though you weren't supposed to. She was pushing the cart and it sounded louder than a train. The wheels kept going all over the place. Her two kids were there, squished into the little seat up front that barely holds one.

"Hi," I said as she passed me.

"Are you with your mother?" she asked. Mrs. Perkins lived three doors down and thought that everything that had anything to do with anyone on our street was her own personal business.

"I'm waiting for a friend of hers."

Mrs. Perkins shook her head and started pushing the cart again. My mother always said that Mrs. P. didn't like us because there wasn't a man in our house. She didn't think that it was right and my mother agreed with her. My mother thought there should be a man in the house, but after my father left she couldn't find one. I think it was because of Rayanne. No good guy would want to live in a house with a retarded kid.

"Who was that?" the guy asked when he got back into the car. "Don't you know not to talk to strangers?" He slammed the door.

"It was Mrs. Perkins. She lives on my street. She has two little kids. She's not a stranger." The guy didn't answer and we drove away real fast.

"I've got a little something for you, Johnny," he said. He pulled a bottle out of a paper bag. "Preventive medicine. You look like you might be coming down with something."

"I feel okay," I said.

"We don't have a spoon, so you'll just have to take it from the bottle cap."

"I'm not sick."

"Look," the guy said. He took his eyes off the road to look at me and the car swerved into the other lane, the wrong-direction lane. "If I tell you to take your medicine,

you take it. I'm not used to children talking back to me.
Your parents might stand for it, but I won't. Got it?"

I wanted to tell him that I didn't have parents, that my
dad didn't even live with us, and didn't he know that, but
I couldn't. It seemed like he was already annoyed with
me. I figured it was because my mother wasn't home, he
couldn't just drop me off, and now he was stuck taking me
everywhere with him.

He put the bottle between his legs and twisted the top
until it opened. "Four capfuls," he said, handing the bottle to me. Even though I felt fine, I did it. It was hard as
hell to pour it in the car and I was scared I'd spill, but I did
it. I swallowed the stuff. Cough medicine, grape only
worse. It tasted like the smell of the stuff my mother used
to polish the furniture. "Good," the guy said. He pulled a
Kit-Kat bar out of his shirt pocket and handed it to me.
"To clear the taste."

We were quiet and he kept driving. It was dark. I
watched the cars coming towards us, two white eyes, staring me down.

"Is my mom home yet?" I asked. I was getting tired.

"I called her from the drugstore and she said not to
bring you home tonight. I think she wanted to be alone."

"What about Rayanne?"

"Alone with Rayanne. She needed you out of her hair
for a while, no big deal."

I shrugged and thought about how much I hated re-
tards, and how they stole the whole show for nothing.

"Where do you live?" I asked.

"We'll be there in a while."

"I'm tired," I said. "And I'm supposed to color maps for
Geography."

"Don't worry, Johnny."

"What's your name?"

"Randy," he said.

And then I don't know what happened. I had my head out the window and felt sick from burgers, fries, shakes, and candy. I was throwing up out the car window while Randy was driving and he didn't even pull over. He didn't put his hand on my forehead like my mother did. He just kept driving and calling me Johnny.

"Wake up, Johnny," Randy said, shaking my shoulder.

It took me a few minutes to get my eyes to stay open, to remember where I was. "Here you go," he said, pushing a spoon of the same grape medicine into my mouth.

"It makes me sick," I said, after I'd swallowed the stuff. I told myself that I'd never swallow it again. I told myself to hold it in my mouth, in my cheek like a hamster, but not to swallow.

"I said you were sick. You didn't listen, did you?" He brought me a glass of water. "Do you want some tea, some toast, some ginger ale?"

I shrugged and felt dizzy.

"You have to eat," he said and then left the room.

I lay in the bed and felt like I would pass out just lying there. I realized that I was almost naked. I wasn't wearing any clothes—except my underwear—and I thought about how my mother told us, especially Rayanne, to be careful of people who might want to mess with you. She said that anyone could be a person who would do a thing like that. She said it might even be someone I knew. She told me this a million times, but never said anything about what if someone took off your clothes while you were asleep. She never mentioned that and still I knew I didn't like it. I sat up and saw my clothes all folded up at the end of the bed. I saw them and thought everything was okay because someone who folds your clothes up and puts them on the end of the bed doesn't seem like the kind of person who would mess with a kid. I reached down, grabbed my clothes, and put them on under the covers.

"Hey, Johnny," Randy said when he came back into the room. He was carrying a tray made out of cardboard. On the tray was a plate of eggs and toast and a glass of juice.

"I'm sick, I can't eat."

"Oh, but you have to eat, you're a growing boy."

"I want to go home."

"Your mother won't want you back if you're sick."

"She'll take care of me."

"Don't be a baby, Johnny."

"Today's my day to collect lunch money," I said.

"You said you were sick. Do you go to school when you're sick? Don't play games with me. Eat your breakfast."

I shook my head.

"What did I tell you to do?" he yelled. The veins in his neck popped out and he went white like sugar. "You do what I tell you and never say no to me, you hear. Never say no to me."

I looked at Randy and thought about how some people were jerks. I thought about how I couldn't wait to be grown up, to have my own private TV, to be alone always. "Now, what did I tell you?"

"Eat the breakfast," I said.

"So do it."

"I'm allergic to eggs." I took small bites of the toast.

"Are you really allergic?" he asked. "Do you want cereal? There are some Rice Krispies in the kitchen. Do you want Krispies?"

"No." I paused. "I want to call my mother and tell her I'm sick. She'll come get me."

"I don't have a phone, Johnny. There isn't a phone."

Randy stood there watching me. He watched everything I did like I was something under a microscope. "Do you like to read?" I shrugged. He pulled a stack of old magazines out from under the bed. "I saved these for you. I have to do some work outside. Is there anything you need?"

"Where's the TV?"

"Don't say television to me. It'll kill you. It makes you so you can't think. Can you think, Johnny?"

I shrugged and he walked out. Randy's magazines were the slippery kind that parents read. They were the kind that Rayanne would spread out all over the floor of the dentist's office and then go skiing on until my mother stopped her. I got out of bed and walked down the hall. The first room was Randy's. It was small and filled with light. There were two windows and a breeze was leaking in from somewhere. The air seemed to spin around, picking up dirt from the floor, making it dance and glow like gold. There was a mattress with green striped sheets, and rows of empty soda bottles, alternating Yahoo, RC, and Mountain Dew, were lined up around the edges of the room, across the windowsill, everywhere. I was in the room, looking, and Randy's hands sank down on my shoulders as if they were taking a bite out of me. He gripped me by the muscle across the top of my back, across my shoulders.

"I was just looking," I said.

"Whose room is this?" he said.

I shrugged.

"Whose?" he asked.

"Yours."

"Did I say you could look? Did I say you could come in here? Did you ask? No!" he yelled into my face. "Some things belong to a person himself. They're private and you can't take them away."

I could smell his breath. It was hot like a dog's. I tried to turn my head away, but he held it straight. He held it with his thumb pressed under my chin.

"You can't have everything. I don't go into your room, looking at your things, do I?"

I wanted to tell him that my room was at home and the room down the hall didn't have anything in it except a bed with blue flowered sheets and a Pepto Bismol–colored blanket. I wanted to tell him that he was starting to remind me of Rayanne because she always asked me to tell her things and then would explain them back to me all wrong.

"You really are a case," he said and then walked out of the room. I followed him down the hall. "Are you a lost dog?" he asked.

"No," I said.

He put his hand on my shoulder and I thought he was going to push me away and say get lost or something. I thought he might crack my head against the wall.

"Are you feeling better, Johnny? Are you ready to go fishing? Do you have a fever?" He pressed his hand up to my forehead, held his palm there for a minute, and then flipped his hand over so that the back side was against my head. I felt his knuckles digging into the thin crevice in the middle of my forehead. "It's gone," he said, taking his hand away and walking farther down the hall.

When his hand was off my head I could still feel the knuckles in that small crack in my skull. I thought about how I'd always figured that gap was a sort of structural deformity. I didn't know it was normal. I thought it was something that could start moving, an earthquake of the mind. I thought the two halves might separate and split my head open. I thought the gap could close and force my brain out through my ears. It always seemed that if anything happened to that place, I'd end up the same as Rayanne. It was like a warning that something could go wrong and I'd be just like my sister. I rubbed my fore-head, letting my fingers dip into that place. I rubbed and wished Randy hadn't touched me there.

"Hey, Johnny, is it time for medicine?"

"I'm fine," I said.

"It's good for you, come on." Randy held out the bottle. His fingers were wrapped around the label. He un-screwed the top and took a small swig, swished it around in his mouth, and swallowed. I shook my head. "I'm not about to force you. That's not what I'm about." He re-capped the bottle and put it down on the ledge above the sink. "My mother used to dose us sometimes. Sometimes at night, she'd want us asleep and we'd still be going full speed and she'd come into the bedroom, hold my nose until my mouth opened, and pour stuff down me; some-times it was brandy, sometimes I didn't know what it was. She always did it to me and not to my brother because he had asthma real bad and she didn't want to mess him up." He paused. "Are you hungry?" I shrugged. Randy opened the refrigerator. "A Fig Newton might work. I'm not a cookie person, but Fig Newtons aren't really cookies, they're more of a medical food, you know? There's milk in here too. There you go, Johnny." He handed me the car-tons.

"I still want to call my mom."

"No phone."

"She's probably wondering where I am."

"No she's not, Johnny. She knows you're with me. I told you that yesterday."

"But aren't I supposed to go home soon? And why don't you have a phone? Everyone has a phone. It's probably illegal not to have one."

"Don't talk law and order to me. Everyone has a phone and a television, and every other one has a video recorder and a washing machine. And then they have microwave ovens. It doesn't mean they're smart. Start collecting things and you get in trouble. You start thinking that you care about the stuff and you forget that it's things, man-made things. It gets like it's a part of you and then it's gone and you feel like you're gone also. When you have stuff and then you don't it's like you've disappeared."

"You have empty bottles in rows all around your room," I said.

"Empties aren't stuff. What are you, stupid?"

"I'm not stupid."

"Keep it that way," Randy said, and then he walked away and I heard the slap of the screen door.

I walked from room to room eating Fig Newtons and drinking milk straight from the carton. I remember thinking it was great that no one was making me pour it into a glass. The rest of the house wasn't much, just a living room with a busted-up sofa and a green chair made out of the same stuff as car seats, the stuff your legs stick to on summer days. I sat down on the sofa and then had to move over to save myself from one of those springs that you can't see but all of the sudden pops through and stabs you in the butt.

I sat there eating cookies and sort of daydreaming. I thought that this was the kind of life I'd live if it was just me and my dad, no mother, no Rayanne. I thought about how everything in our house got all weird when my dad came to visit. My mother would run around putting everything into piles on top of the TV or the coffee table. Then she'd go to the grocery store and buy things like broccoli and veal chops. We'd have to put clean clothes on and sit with her in the living room until she heard his truck coming down the street, the gears shifting down. My father would come into the house and we'd be standing there like we were in the army and you could tell from his face that he wished he hadn't come. It was like he wanted to sneak in and have us find him sitting there watching TV like he'd never been gone. It was like he made himself think that he didn't matter, that his leaving didn't matter. Sometimes he'd try and fake us out. He'd drop by without warning. Rayanne, my mom, and I might be out in the front yard and we'd hear the truck as soon as it turned the corner at the end of the street. Rayanne would look up and see him sitting twenty feet up in the cab and she'd take off, galloping towards the truck in her retarded way, legs getting tangled in each other, never sure which foot should go next.

The screen door slapped shut and somewhere in my head I heard it, but didn't really know where I was. I was still thinking about my father, his truck, and the view from up in the cab.

"Hey, hey, Johnny," Randy said. "Are you sleeping?"

"Not exactly," I mumbled.

"What exactly?"

I shrugged.

"You don't have to spend all day in the house. When I saw you out there playing ball, I figured you were an outdoor type."

I shook my head.

"I like to watch TV. I watch TV and my sister comes in. I can't stand her, so sometimes I have to get out of the house. My sister is retarded, did you know that?"

Randy nodded.

"No matter how old she gets, she'll never be better than a seven-year-old. She calls my father Uncle because she says that daddies live at home and uncles just come and visit."

"Yeah, well, get up. We're going fishing. What we catch is what we eat for dinner."

"I don't know how to fish."

"I'll teach you, Johnny."

I shrugged.

"Do you care about anything?"

I shrugged again.

"Don't shrug. Either talk or don't, but don't goddamn shrug at me. It's like saying go to hell, only worse. You're saying it's not even worth the energy it takes to say the words."

I walked through the woods behind Randy.

"The trick," he said, "is just like life. Don't let them know you want them. Play dumb and they'll act dumb."

He pushed the boat into the water and we waded in. My jeans got wet up to my thighs and felt like weights wrapped around my legs. Randy rowed out into the lake. He handed me a coffee can. "Take one out and put it right there on the end."

I looked into the can and saw about a thousand worms. "I can't," I said.

"You can and you will," Randy said, holding out the hook to me. He talked in the same tone my mother used with Rayanne when she wanted her to do something. "We can sit here until the moon is blue."

I turned my head away and put my hand into the can. The thin rolls of worm were soft and a little silky. They were stuck together, piled on top of one another. I had to look directly into the can in order to pick one up. I handed it to Randy.

"On the hook," he said. "Put it on the hook." I jammed it down on the hook, ripping its body, squirting worm juice into the air.

Randy cast the fishing line out over the lake, explaining how it was all in the flick of the wrist. He handed me the pole and I looked out at the thin plastic line. I looked across the lake and saw a man on the other side. I got up on my knees, nearly dropped the fishing pole, and waved. I kept doing it until Randy slapped my hand down. But the man across the lake had seen me. He waved back and then Randy had to wave to get him to stop waving.

"People here like to be left alone," Randy said. "You shouldn't have bothered him."

I started crying, not out loud, but to myself. I was crying and thinking about how I wanted to go home, put on dry clothes, talk to my mom, and watch TV.

"What's with you, Johnny? It's a beautiful day, you're out fishing, you've never fished before, but you're doing it, and you're acting worse than an old hat."

There was a yank on my line and I sat up.

"Pull back slowly, just a little bit."

I did what he said.

"Don't let him think he's caught. If he thinks he can get away he'll try and wait you out. But if you let him know he's caught, he'll fight like hell."

We pulled him in and then the fish was there, hanging from the hook, staring at me. Randy dropped him onto the floor of the boat. The fish flopped around.

"Say hello to dinner," Randy said.

"I'm not eating."

"You'll eat."

I shook my head.

"Bait another hook."

I watched the fish until its gills stopped flapping, until I was sure it was dead. I watched for about ten minutes and then jammed another worm onto the hook. Randy got a bite on his line and pulled in a small fish. He took it off the hook and threw it back into the water. "I'm not a murderer, Johnny," he said.

When we had three fish Randy put away the poles and

we ate sandwiches right there in the boat with the fish at our feet. "This is the life," Randy said.

I could feel the sun on the place on my shoulder where Randy had grabbed me when I was in his room. I could feel the sun through my shirt and it was like hands rubbing a sore place. I leaned back in the boat and used one of the floating cushions as a pillow.

"Hey, hey, Johnny, wake up." Randy had rowed us back to shore. "You sleep a lot for a kid your age."

"It's because of being sick."

"You were out all afternoon and you didn't seem sick. It's all in your head. You're sick in the head."

I got out of the boat and helped pull it back into the woods. "Last night you said I was sick. I threw up."

"I didn't know you like I do today." He paused. "Pregnant ladies throw up—are they sick? It's your head, Johnny."

Randy cooked the fish for dinner. We ate and then I helped him clean up.

"My father's coming to visit soon and I have to be there," I said. "It's the law. My mother lines us up by the piano and I have to be there."

"Johnny, she knows where you are. If she wanted you, she'd come get you."

The morning after that Randy woke me up, told me to hurry, handed me a cream cheese sandwich, and said I'd have to eat it in the car.

"Where are we going?"

"Did you ever split wood?" he asked.

"I've peeled the bark off branches."

"Ever hold an axe?"

"No."

Randy drove to a small shopping center and pulled in

near the hardware store. There was a 7-Eleven right next to the hardware store with a pay phone in front. I followed Randy into the hardware store, but put my hand in my pocket and felt around for a quarter. While Randy was talking to the guy about axes and wedges I pretended to get lost looking for some fishing stuff. I went outside to the pay phone, put the quarter in, and dialed. I dialed my mother and waited. I thought Randy was going to come outside and kill me. I thought he'd come out with an axe and take off my head. I didn't care. The phone clicked a couple of times and then beeped busy. A couple of people came out of the 7-Eleven and I thought of asking them for help, but I wasn't sure what I'd say. I put the quarter in again and dialed. Busy. I hung up, got the quarter back, and put it in again. It started to ring, but then I thought I'd dialed the wrong number. I only had one quarter and I thought I might have hit an eight and not a five. I hung up, put the quarter in, and dialed again. Still busy. I thought of calling the operator or the police. I hung up, dialed again. Randy came out of the store and saw me at the phone. He was carrying the axe in one hand and a package in the other.

"What are you doing?" he asked.

"Trying to call my mom."

"Any luck?"

"Line's busy."

He came over to the telephone and just stood there. He didn't get mad. He didn't kill me. He just stood there, listening to the phone beep. "Try again," he said.

I hung up, put the quarter back in, and dialed again. Busy. "Why is she on the phone?"

"Talking to someone," Randy said. He leaned against the wall of the 7-Eleven like he was going to stay there all day. He leaned back like he didn't care that I was calling home.

I felt like an idiot with him standing there, not trying to stop me. I felt mentally ill. Randy was telling the truth; my mother wasn't worried. She was sitting home, talking on the telephone.

"Let's go," I finally said.

"Go on, give it another try." I almost put the quarter in again, but then I wondered what I would say. What could I say with Randy right there, telling me to go ahead and call? I put the quarter into my pocket.

We went home and Randy showed me how to split logs; how to swing the axe with both arms straight, to swing up over my shoulder and then go straight down into the log. He explained about putting in the metal wedges so that with a few whacks the whole piece split open like an English muffin.

When we were done, Randy showed me how to cook; we made sandwiches and Rice Krispie squares. Then we went into the living room, ate, played poker, and passed a carton of milk back and forth between us. Sometimes when I drank, I'd tilt the carton a little too high and milk spilled out onto my face, ran back behind my ear and down my neck.

"A kid like you should have more to say," Randy said. "You should be nonstop, filled with ideas, things you're going to do, all that stuff."

I didn't look at him.

"It's like you're not all there," he said.

I was looking at the dirt in the cracks on the floor. Randy said it was like I wasn't all there and I thought about Rayanne and wondered if she had lots of things trapped in her head. I thought about how she didn't really understand how retarded she was and how she thought I was a genius or something. I thought maybe I was like her, not enough for everyone to notice but enough for a guy like Randy to catch on. I thought it was probably my parents' fault for not telling me. Maybe that's why my father left. Maybe my mother, Rayanne, and me were all the same; maybe we were all retarded.

"Are you sleeping, Johnny?" Randy asked.

I shook my head.

"What's wrong with you?"

I shrugged and waited for him to hit me. The Krispie pan was on the coffee table with a couple of pieces left in it. The milk carton was right there too. I reached my foot out and with the tip of my sneaker tipped the pan over. I knocked the pan over right in front of Randy.

He just sat there and looked at me. His face didn't change. "Feel better now?" he finally asked, sweeping the cards into a pile and then making them into a stack. I shrugged. He stood and I shriveled up. I didn't mean to, but he was standing over me and that's just what happened. "Don't be scared of me, Johnny," he said. "Be scared of yourself." He picked up the milk carton and took it into the kitchen. I heard the refrigerator door open and close. I heard Randy pull out a chair and sit down. I got up off the sofa and onto my hands and knees. I picked up the pan, took it into the kitchen, and put it down on the counter.

" 'Night, Johnny," Randy said. He was playing solitaire.

" 'Night." I walked down the hall to my room.

The next morning Randy was gone. I sat on the living room sofa and waited. I went outside and sat on the concrete front step. Across the dirt that was the front yard there were still pieces of wood that needed to be split and stacked. I picked up the axe. It felt heavier than I remembered. I raised it and went to work. About a half hour later Randy drove up.

"Where'd you go?" I asked.

He shrugged. "Put shoes on," he said. "Never work out-side without shoes."

I followed him into the house. "I'm sorry for what I did last night," I said. I'd been rehearsing it in my head all morning.

He nodded.

I went down the hall to get my shoes. Randy was in the kitchen making eggs for himself. "I said I was sorry."

"I hear you." He scraped the eggs out of the pan and onto a plate. I kept looking at him and he looked back at me. "Did you finish all the wood?" I shook my head. Randy started to eat and I went outside and kept splitting and stacking.

When the wood was chopped I went into my room and fell asleep. The slap-slapping sound of a basketball woke me up. Randy was dribbling down the hall. He stood in the doorway bouncing the ball. "Get up, Johnny," he said. "We're going."

"Where?"

He shrugged and threw the ball at me, hard.

I caught it. It was my ball. I hadn't seen it since the night Randy picked me up. I held the ball for a minute and then put it down on the bed.

"Take it with you," he said.

I followed him out to the car. "Do you know how to drive?"

"I'm way too young."

"Never too young." He moved the car seat as far for-ward as it would go. If I sat so I could see, my legs were nowhere near the pedals. "You're too short," Randy said. I slid over so he could drive. He pulled the seat release and the whole front seat slid backwards.

"Let's go fishing again," I said.

"I don't think so, Johnny," he said and I was quiet for a long time. The road turned into highway and I could feel him making the car go faster. It was afternoon. The sun was starting to go down.

"Where are we going?" I asked.

He didn't say anything for a while. "You're not the kid I thought you'd be."

"What does that mean?"

He turned off the highway and we were someplace I'd been before. I turned the basketball around on my lap.

"I'm taking you back," he said. He made a few turns and I knew where he was.

"What's wrong with me?"

"You're not the right kid. You're not Johnny." Randy pulled up to the curb right at the bottom of the hill below the basketball courts. This was the exact same place he'd parked when he came up to the courts and called me Johnny. "Get out," he said. I sat there looking at the dashboard. "You've spent three days whining about calling your mother and going home. Now you're home. Go on, get out."

"Why?"

He leaned across me and opened the door on my side of the car.

"Out," he said, shoving my shoulder.

I got out.

Randy pulled away from the curb, turned the car around, and went back down the hill.

I walked home, cutting through the same backyards as always. I walked the same way but everything felt different. All the things I'd always liked, knowing who lived where and what their dog's name was, only made me feel worse. I went past clotheslines and instead of thinking it was funny to see Mrs. Perkins's flowered underwear hanging out, I wanted to rip it down. I wanted to take everything down and tear it into a million pieces. I crossed through the Simons' yard and into our backyard.

Rayanne was there by herself, playing in my sandbox. She was thirteen years old, bigger than my mother, and she was playing in the sandbox. I stood there until she saw me. She looked at me and tried to jump up. She wanted to get up but she did it too fast and didn't know what she was doing. She fell down and had to get up again. "Erol, Erol," she said, galloping across the backyard. "Erol," she said, but it came out sounding like "Error, Error." She came towards me and I dropped my basketball. I turned and ran back through the yards. I ran until I didn't know the names of the people in the houses around me. I ran through backyards until I stopped hearing Rayanne's voice calling Error.

CHUNKY IN HEAT

Her thighs spread across the vinyl ropes of the lawn chair. In the heat they seem to melt into the plastic, seeping out from under her shorts, slipping through the vinyl as though eventually she'll begin dripping fat onto the lawn.

"Chunky?" her mother calls through the sliding glass door. The voice is muffled and sounds like a drowning person talking under water. "I'm running errands, are you coming with me?"

Cheryl shakes her head. Her second chin rolls across her chest, gliding on a layer of sweat.

"Why not?"

Her mother seems to be gurgling behind the glass.

Cheryl doesn't answer.

"I'm leaving now," her mother says, and then waits at the glass for several minutes before walking away.

Cheryl lays on the chair in the center of the backyard, her right hand plucking individual blades of grass, her eyes not focused but aimed at a bald spot of lawn, a remnant from another afternoon when she had a similar problem.

They call her Chunky in part after the candy bar, which used to be her favorite. Her mother started it.

Cheryl was eating a bar and refused to give some to her little brother. "Too small to share," she said, popping it all into her mouth, ending the discussion.

He called her Fatty and poked her in the stomach; his finger sank deep into her flesh.

"Your sister is just chunky," her mother said.

"You bet she is," he said.

After that he called her Chunky and then everyone called her Chunky, and then as if being called Chunky actually made her fatter, she truly was Chunky—and she hated that candy bar and switched to Mr. Goodbar but didn't tell anybody.

Cheryl is fat, only she didn't know it until now. Before this she always thought of herself as a big girl, a growing girl, a girl who could do anything. Now, in the heat, in the sun, she lies immobile and swollen. She feels larger and larger as if her breath is actually inflating her. She tries not to breathe as much, as deeply. Her double chin presses down onto her chest, onto her windpipe, and she feels like she is suffocating. Cheryl tilts her head back, establishing an airway.

She tilts her head and thinks of models in *Vogue* who seem like they can tilt anything, like they aren't people but fully articulated dolls like her brother's G.I. Joe—G.I. Joke she calls him. She thinks of thin people on beaches, with a breeze slipping over them. She realizes that because they are thin, they are aerodynamic. She pictures herself on the sand and sees a blob exactly like a jellyfish.

Two incredibly large insects, with wing spans like small airplanes, buzz past Cheryl. They buzz back and forth within a foot of her head, and on their second pass-by they lock together belly to belly like Siamese twins. Their wings beat against each other with a faint clicking sound. They are mating; Cheryl knows that. She knows what they are doing, but she doesn't know how. She doesn't know what they are doing it with. She can't see anything. The insects' green eyes bulge out of the sockets, their front feelers claw at each other, and Cheryl feels sick. There are too many sensations, too many distractions. She is writhing in her lawn chair, shifting her limbs, her balance. The chair rocks and lifts into the air as if it might tip and dump Cheryl onto the grass. She grips the armrests, thinking that holding tight will make her safe.

"I'm gonna get you, I'm gonna get you." Cheryl hears the voice of her next-door neighbor. "Oooh, I'm gonna get you now." There is a high-pitched scream, a squeal of pleasure. Her next-door neighbor is chasing his daughter around in the backyard. She is six years old. "Bet you can't get me. Bet you can't," she mimics and taunts her father.

"Oooh, I'm gonna."

"Enough," the mother screams and then there is silence.

Cheryl looks around the yard and back at the house. Everything is still and shadowless as if stunned by the heat, the light, and the peak of the day. The house appears flat, as if it's been cut out from a magazine and glued back into another picture. Even with the fence around it and the ivy from the neighbors' yard growing over, wrapping around like guy wires, it is as if at any moment the house might take off and disappear into the wild blue yonder. There are no anchors, no signs of life, no swing set, pool, barbecue, nothing except Cheryl in the backyard.

She looks at the house, but focuses on the sensations of herself in the heat, of her clothing in the heat, against her body. Cheryl wears her clothing like the protective coating on a cold capsule. Clothing divides her body into reasonable sections, arms and legs that need to be kept apart from other arms and legs, safe from the possibility of skin touching skin and rubbing itself raw.

Outside, as she sweats, her clothing separates itself

from her body and begins to slip slightly, working against her, moving independently. When she breathes in, her bra creeps up and sticks, like a rubber band around her ribs, biting her and then creeping up again, higher, when she exhales.

In a moment of extreme consciousness, she sits straight up, reaches her hand up the back of her shirt, and releases the bra, sending it snapping across her chest like a slingshot. She pulls it off under her shirt and drops it, lifeless, onto the grass.

In the hot air the surface of her skin becomes tacky and the tops of her thighs touch and stick together, gripping each other in a vaguely masturbatory manner. She moves her legs to separate them. This touching and pulling apart causes a soft lip-smacking sound. Her thighs rub together even in her thoughts.

There is the distant sound of a doorbell, a sound like the tone in a hearing test. When you hear the beep, raise your finger. She hears the doorbell and then a muffled voice.

"Chunky, Chunky, are you here?"

She hears the boy who lives next door, the boy who is three years younger than her, the boy she plays games with that they tell no one about. She does it because he wants to and she wants to and she can't find anyone her own age to do it with and besides she feels better doing it with him because she's bigger than him, and he does what she tells him to. He doesn't care that she's fat because he's getting to and he doesn't know anyone else who is getting to, and he likes that she is older because even though he can't talk about it anywhere, it gives him a new kind of credibility even if it's only in his mind. She doesn't let him see her actually naked; that's one of her rules and part of what makes it all right. He just sees bits and pieces but it's never too much, never overwhelming. He doesn't try to kiss her and she likes that.

"Chunky, are you here?" His voice is higher than it should be. She doesn't like it when he talks. "Chunky, I think you're home."

She hears him calling but doesn't answer. It doesn't mean she doesn't want him, but she can't bring herself to speak. She lies on the lawn chair and thinks of him coming around the house, into the backyard and finding her. She thinks of him topless, his shoulders looking new and too big for the rest of him. She sees him unzipping his shorts and pulling them down, his erection jutting forward like an extra limb, a birth defect. She spreads her legs and he comes towards her. She has to spread her legs very wide in order to make a space between her thighs. He kneels on the grass and pushes in.

He grabs her breasts and squeezes them again and again like they are the black rubber bulbs on bicycle horns. He pushes into her hard and quick and she can feel it everywhere. He slams in and the newest part of her, the freshest fat, the softest flesh, jiggles. Her hips, thighs, and butt jiggle. Her breasts jiggle each time and she loves it; she loves the jiggling.

This is the thing about being fat that no one mentions. Everything feels good, every square inch has incredible sensations, as if skin when stretched becomes hypersensitive, as if by stretching the skin to cover the fat the nerves become exposed or sharpened: it is not just her flesh rubbing against itself but the very sensation of its existence, hanging from her body, apart from her body, swaying, jiggling, touching things.

"Chunky, are you in there? If you don't answer I'm leaving."

She imagines him not on top of her, but apart from her except in that one place and every time he goes in she slides up on the sweaty vinyl so that when they finish her head is hanging off the end and he can barely reach her.

She imagines him and as she imagines him she slips her hand into her shorts. She imagines him and she pulls her shorts down to her knees. She digs her heels into the bottom of the chair and pushes up, raising her butt up off the chair. Her flesh pulls up and off the chair like adhesive tape being removed and it hurts a little and she likes the sting and repeats the thrusting until her skin is raw and sweat coats the chair like butter and she doesn't stick anymore. She pulls her shirt up to her neck so her nipples can get the air.

When she finishes and realizes she is half-naked, her pants caught at her knees, her shirt at her throat, the sensation of being outside, in the middle of the day where someone might see her—and suddenly she feels like someone, at least one person, is seeing her with her clothes all pushed up and pulled down—is too much and she has to do it again, this time more slowly, this time for an audience. This time, she pulls all her clothing off. She does it lying on her back, imagining someone seeing her doing it. All she's thinking about is people watching and she's not fat or thin, she's sex, pure sex, and as they're watching her she thinks they're probably doing it too and she likes that.

She remembers when she was a little girl, maybe five, her mother walked into her room and Cheryl was on her bed with her pants pulled down and her butt poked up in the air. Even then she liked to get the air inside her, on her.

"What are you doing?" her mother asked.

Even then Cheryl didn't answer.

She remembers feeling something more than embarrassed but she can't think of the word. Cheryl is getting too old for this. She is so old that it is embarrassing.

Cheryl is naked on her lounge chair. Her mother comes home. Cheryl hears the car in the driveway on the other side of the house. She hears the fan running, the a/c still on, and then she hears the car turn off and the fan is still going. The car door opens and does not close, and suddenly everything is all wrong.

Her mother slides the screen door open and calls "Chunky" without looking at her daughter. "Chunky, Chunky, I'm calling you," her mother says, without noticing Cheryl white and naked, lying like a beached whale. "Chunky."

Cheryl is trapped in her head. She is aware of herself naked in the yard, naked in the day. She is aware of her name being called.

She imagines her mother will go back in the house and dial 911. She will dial 911 and report that her sixteen-year-old fat daughter is lying naked in the family backyard on a chair from K-mart and fails to respond when her name is called.

"Sweetie," her mother says, and Cheryl wonders how many calories are in the word *sweetie* and then she realizes that it's just a word and it's fat-free.

"I went to the grocery store, do you want to help me unpack?"

Her mother says, do you want to help me, and she means it. She is perfectly willing to do it alone, but she wants Cheryl to know that if she wants too, if she'd like to do something other than sit naked in the yard, she can come in and help, but she is under no obligation. It is simply an option.

Cheryl likes unpacking. She likes opening things and, before putting them away, tasting just a little bit.

She stands up, peeling herself off the lawn chair with a long sucking sound, and walks towards the house. As she walks, her legs slip past each other with the same whooshing sound that corduroy makes. Her breasts and belly and butt bounce as she walks; they bounce with different beats but all in some strange syncopation, like a strung-out rhythm section.

She steps over the threshold. The contrast between light outside and the darkness inside makes the dark somehow darker and causes temporary blindness. For the first minute all she can see is the front door, straight ahead across the living room. It is open. She can see out into the light. She thinks of walking through the house and out the other side. The darkness seems to take her over, to swallow her. She stands still. There are mirrors on both sides of the living room walls. She sees herself as a large mass of unbelievable whiteness. She sees her shape, the scope of herself and her size. She feels deformed.

In the air conditioning she can feel herself shrinking, somehow getting smaller all over. She looks away from the mirrors and focuses ahead on the open door. Her mother is just outside bringing in bags from the car. The boy from next door passes by on his skateboard and looks in the door. He sees her and calls out her name, "Chunky." Cheryl stands there, sees him see her, hears her name, and still stands there. Without realizing it she drops her hand to her crotch, covering herself. Her mother comes in carrying three bags, looks at her, and says, "Get dressed, dear."

JIM TRAIN

It is Jim's idea to walk every day to and from the station. He thinks of leaving his new home, walking down the sidewalks, past the neighbors' homes, over the small bridge to the train station as a pleasant thing to do, the kind of thing he imagines would keep a man alive.

"It gives me time to think," he tells anyone who asks why he doesn't just have his wife drop him off at the station like all the other men.

"I enjoy large thoughts," he says to his wife one evening. "I need them now. My thoughts are my food," he says. "I have to eat."

Jim pops a section of a Ho-Ho into his mouth; cream filling squirts out onto his lips.

"I understand," his wife says, refusing to look at him. The sight of food in a person's mouth makes her ill. "Good night." She turns off the lamp on her side of the bed.

In the morning as he walks, Jim passes unoccupied cars, motors running, warming up, spilling thick exhaust out onto the sidewalks, into the air. He steers around them fully realizing that avoiding the smoke means nothing, toxicity surrounds him.

He weaves down the sidewalk, briefcase in hand,

sweating lightly in his overcoat, feeling young, like a boy, looking forward to school and at the same time drawing out his walk so that inevitably he always arrives at the last minute.

On his way into town, he reviews his thoughts, which frequently come to him in the form of a speech. Each day he either adds or subtracts something so that by the time he reaches the station, he has relieved his mind to the extent that when the train pulls in and he squeezes himself into a seat, holding his briefcase on his lap—the weight and trapped heat lowering what is left of his sperm count—he quickly falls asleep.

Jim is a lawyer, as is everyone in New York City, or so it seems. His office is on the thirty-fourth floor of a large midtown office tower. Every morning his first activity after being greeted by his secretary—who bounds towards him, messages in hand, with all the good cheer of a well-bred retriever—is to close his door and call home.

"I'm here," he says, as soon as either his wife or the housekeeper picks up the phone.

"Good," the voice on the other end is trained to say.

"Great," Jim says. "Gotta go."

Occasionally when he calls, there is no answer, and Jim gets nervous. His palms sweat, and he finds it difficult to breathe. He sits paralyzed at his desk and pushes the redial button every two minutes until finally someone picks up. It is all he can do to stop himself from hitting redial every minute, or thirty seconds. This did not happen years ago, before they moved out of town. After all, before, if his wife was not home, she was out there somewhere, perhaps walking just below his office window. Now, if she is not home, she is *truly* out there, easily miles from home, possibly in another state.

Each evening, well past eight, when all the offices are

empty, Jim goes down the hall, leans back in the senior partner's chair, and looks out over the Manhattan skyline. He relaxes for fifteen or twenty minutes and then on his way out he peeks into the hall, making sure the cleaning lady is at the far end of the floor, unzips his fly, and relieves himself into the large potted plant Patterson keeps by the door.

It is Jim's rule that except in cases of extreme emergency, he is not permitted to pee between lunch and the end of the day. By eight o'clock he has collected a sufficient quantity of urine. It is his ritual, his salvation.

Since signing on with Flynch, Peabody, and Patterson, Jim's lost count of how many plants he's killed. Patterson's secretary seems to think their death has to do with the lack of light, the poor quality of air in the building, or possibly a high concentration of lead in the drinking water. The associates make jokes about the horrible smell by Patterson's door. In one the punch line is something about how it's better to drop dead in your tracks than go dripping off like the old man, who in reality is hardly old.

"Not interrupting you, am I?" Patterson says as he walks into Jim's office, laughing, fully aware that there is no such thing as the senior partner interrupting anyone. "You're Flynch-Peabody's Man of the Year."

Jim doesn't know what he's talking about. He feels like a surprise contestant on a game show.

Patterson's secretary comes in with a plaque the size of a coffee table. Patterson himself is grinning from ear to ear. A photographer rushes in and snaps a few pictures of Patterson and Jim standing with the plaque between them. Jim's secretary carries in a large potted plant. Jim blushes deep red and feels his knees turn into rubber bands.

This is a joke, a bad joke, Jim thinks. This is Flynch-Peabody's way of saying good-bye.

"You should be proud," Patterson says, shaking Jim's hand. "Not every man is Man of the Year. I never was. Don't think I don't know you're here every night after everyone leaves. I have my spies." He winks at Jim and then leaves.

"Congratulations," Jim's secretary says, still holding the potted plant, which must weigh at least forty pounds. "Where should we put it?"

"Take it home," Jim says. "I have terrible allergies."

His secretary carries the plant out to her desk and Jim calls home again. The line is busy.

The shock of the award, the plant in particular, has left him weak. He's still seeing the blue spots from the photographer's flash in front of his eyes. There is no way he can work.

"Early lunch appointment, slipped my mind," Jim says as he passes his secretary's desk on his way out.

I am a self-made man, he tells himself in the elevator. He looks into the silver polish of the control panel and sees his reflection, distorted. I made you and I can break you, any time I want. Something to keep in mind, buddy boy.

Jim takes a long walk, circling the block twice, picking up the power to go farther, then heading in the direction of the river. He thinks about his job, about the view from Patterson's big chair, about how good it feels to finally let go when you've been holding it in all afternoon. Within a half hour, Jim is so fully revived that he marches back to the office.

There are police cars and fire engines everywhere. The

street has been sealed off and is filled with people. Jim is panicked and dizzy. No one seems to know what the situation is. He finally spots his secretary, standing tall above the crowd.

"I'm so glad you're all right," she says.

"What's going on?" Jim asks.

"Bomb threat," his secretary says.

Jim sees Mr. Patterson leaning on a police car and goes to him.

"Train, Train, I'm so glad they found you," Patterson says. "That's it then, we're all out."

"Is there really a bomb?"

Patterson looks grim. "Could be," he says. "Don't really know. We've got a couple of difficult cases coming up, could be related. Remember Wertheimer?" Patterson says, referring to someone who was let go under strange circumstances a few months earlier. "Could be Wertheimer. You never know what a man will do." Patterson nods, tapping his fingers to his head, indicating the possibility of insanity. Train nods vigorously along with Patterson. "Go home," Patterson says. "Call it a day."

Jim shakes his head. "My briefcase is inside. I've got calls to make."

"Go on," Patterson says, flicking his fingers as if shooing Jim away. "Go home."

Jim lingers. He doesn't want to go home. He wants to go to work. He is the Man of the Year. His plaque is up there on the thirty-fourth floor, just next to his desk. He has to decide where to hang it. Jim walks down Lexington Avenue to Forty-second Street, feeling rejected, disconcerted by the absence of his jacket and briefcase.

He thinks of a bomb and imagines it buried in Patterson's plant, launching the tall tropical wonder like a missile. The plant crashes through a single window on the thirty-fourth floor as though heaved in anger. A second later all the windows blow out, and a ball of orange fire claims the floor. *Whoosh,* the world is up in smoke.

Jim takes the two-forty train home and walks up the sidewalks, warm and clear with afternoon sun. The streets are full of station wagons, carpools going in all directions. He has the clear impression from the looks drivers give him that the sidewalks are not intended for use by anyone except women with strollers and children under twelve.

He passes the spastic boy that he sees every evening, except in foul weather. The boy is never out in the mornings and Jim imagines that because of his twisted shape it takes a very long time to get him dressed and fed. He stands in matching pants and shirt at the foot of his parents' driveway, frozen in a bent, painful pose, giving Jim a clear idea of what a cast-iron jockey would look like if it were struck by a car or truck.

The boy sees Jim and waves. Jim waves back. He never speaks because he's afraid the boy will talk to him and perhaps he won't understand what the boy is saying and then it will get complicated and even more depressing, so he leaves it at the waving.

On this occasion Jim worries that perhaps he has confused the boy by coming home early and maybe the boy will do something like go inside expecting dinner to be served. Perhaps his mother will think his action is proof of her suspicion that he's regressing and that he really is getting too old and difficult for her to care for and before supper she will call the institution and arrange for them to come and collect him by morning.

Jim has the urge to go back down the block and explain his arrival, but the idea of explaining is too exhausting and he resigns himself to feeling guilty.

Jim's key doesn't open the door. Instantly, he's afraid that he has walked to the wrong house, he has forgotten his own address, he will become like the spastic boy and stand frozen at the end of the driveway until someone, his wife he hopes, drives by and recognizes him.

He goes from the kitchen door to the front door and back again. He jumps up and looks in the window and feels comforted when he sees his loafers lying empty in the hall. The familiarity of his belongings and the sensation of being separated from them make him that much more determined to get inside. He breaks the key in half trying to work the lock open.

"Shit," he says.

"Hello?"

He hears his neighbor's voice through the bushes at the end of the driveway.

"Is someone there?"

He doesn't answer. He sits on the steps as though he's been sent out as punishment. He is alone in what he thinks of as the middle of nowhere. For five minutes he just sits there, his knees up to his chest, poking the plastic ends of his shoelaces into the eyelets on his shoes, resting.

This would never have happened on 87th Street. He would have gone downstairs and gotten the extra key from the super. He would have run around the corner to the Pearlmans' and waited there in the comfort of their living room. Jim is living in the past, a place where his memory tells him life was easier, almost effortless.

Jim removes his tie and goes into the backyard in his pink oxford-cloth shirt and gray flannel pants. He relieves himself in an azalea bush but it is boring, like being on a camping trip. Little green shoots are poking up all over the yard. His children have left a trowel and a hand rake in the dirt by the driveway and it occurs to Jim that weeding will make him feel better; it will divert his anxious energy. It will make him a farmer, a man he has never been before.

He gets down on his hands and knees and begins digging, pulling green things out of the dirt. He makes three stacks of weed balls and is in the process of making a turban out of his shirt when a car pulls into the driveway. He runs around the side of the house, joyous that his family has returned, his shirt wrapped loosely around his head, the sleeves hanging down like floppy ears.

Bill's Repair Man looks at him as though there's some sort of a problem. His expression causes Jim to look down at himself. He's covered with dirt. Clumps of soil are embedded in his chest hair. His gray flannels have grass stains unlike any seen in detergent commercials. One pant leg is ripped open at the knee, the skin under it raw, from when Jim accidently kneeled down hard on a buried rock.

"Doing a little planting?" the repair man asks.

The name sewn on his uniform says Bob even though the truck says Bill. Jim figures that Bob must work for Bill, perhaps they're even related.

"Weeding actually," Jim says, relishing the sensation of explaining himself to a guy with his name sewn on his shirt who clearly doesn't know putting in from taking out, planting from weeding.

"I'm here to fix the hot water heater," Bob says.

"There's a little difficulty with the door," Jim says. "My key broke off in the lock."

"Which door?" Bob says.

Jim points up to the kitchen door, and the repair man takes his toolbox out of the truck. Jim follows him up the stairs. Just as they're getting the door open, Jim's wife pulls up in the car. Susan seems surprised by the sight of him and Jim's not sure if it's because he's home hours earlier than usual, or if it's the shirt on his head and the dirt on his chest that have thrown her off guard.

"Daddy!" His daughter Emily hurls herself at him, hugging his knees.

"Did you bring me anything?" his older child, Jake, asks.

"Just me," Jim says.

Jake makes a face. He sees the weeds that Jim dug up lying in a heap by the driveway.

"You're in trouble now," Jake says.

"You idiot," Susan screams as she rounds the edge of the car and looks into the backyard. "You dug up my marigolds." She runs through the yard shouting. "What the hell is wrong with you? Are you insane?" Jim charges down the steps and into the yard. He's almost willing to kill Susan to keep the neighbors from hearing her.

"Be quiet," he says loudly. "Be quiet."

"You ruined my garden, you fool," Susan screams and then stands silent in the middle of the yard, her arms crossed over her chest.

Bill's Repair Man comes out of the house to get something from his truck. He's grinning and Jim has the urge to punch him, but his children are staring at him, waiting to see what an adult does after being completely humiliated.

Jim walks past all of them, up the steps, and into his house.

There's no reason I should know what a marigold is, he thinks, I'm the Flynch-Peabody Man of the Year.

He goes up to the bedroom, empties the contents of the hamper onto the bed, spreads the dirty clothing out evenly, and lies down on top of it. He stares up at the ceiling, sucking his thumb, and occasionally rubbing a soft piece of clothing across his face. This is something he does to relax. He doesn't think it is any stranger than a person taking a Valium, lifting weights, or immersing himself in some kind of tank. Emily comes in with her bottle and lies down next to him.

"You're dirty," Emily says.

Jim nods.

"It's okay." She rests her head on his chest, sucks her bottle, and falls asleep.

The phone rings, Jim gets up carefully, so as not to disturb Emily, and picks up the phone in the hall.

"Hi, it's Bill MacArthur."

"Oh, hi Bill, how are you?" Susan says, from the extension in the kitchen.

Jim tries to remember who this Bill is. In the six months they've lived there he's met four Bills, two Bobs, three Roberts, and a Robbie, and he can't tell one from the other.

"Good, good," Bill says. "I'm just getting ready to run the kids down to the park and toss around the ball. I thought maybe you'd like to bring yours."

"What a nice idea."

Jim knows that if he'd gone downstairs a minute before and said, Honey, let's take the kids to the park and toss a ball around, she would have looked at him like he was crazy.

"I'll stop by and you can follow me in your car."

Jim tries to imagine who Bill MacArthur is. What's his relation to the real MacArthur? Doesn't he have a job? A family, his own damn wife?

"Kids, kids, where are you?" Susan calls, as she runs up the steps. "Get your shoes on, we're going to the park."

"Can I come with you?" Jim asks, as Susan rubs a damp washcloth over Emily's face, wiping off her sleep and the dirt from Jim's chest.

"You have to stay home and re-plant my flowers."

Jim feels as if he's been slam-dunked. How can he do anything when she's running off into the woods chasing wild balls with some guy named Bill?

"Do you wear your ring?" he asks.

"What ring?" Susan says.

"You know, your ring?" Jim spins his wedding band around.

"Oh that ring. You scared me for a minute. Of course, except when I'm doing the dishes. What makes you ask?"

MacArthur's horn beeps in front of the house.

Jim stands on the landing, looking out the window. He tries to wave to Bill MacArthur, whoever the hell he is, but MacArthur doesn't see him.

Jim decides to take a shower outside, it will save him the job of cleaning the tub when he's done. He takes a towel and a bar of soap and goes into the yard, hauling the hose after him.

This is what men who don't live in cities do, he thinks, imagining naked men in backyards all over Westchester and up into Connecticut. They shower out-of-doors, like Abe Lincoln. It's the hearty way. The real way.

He picks at the dirt embedded in his chest hair, and rubs what he gets between his fingers. He throws the hose over a tree branch and turns on the water—it is cool if not cold. Jim starts to sing. He lathers himself from head to toe, watching the dirt pour off his body in little muddy rivers. He rinses his hair and, when the soap is out of his eyes, looks into the bushes at the far end of the yard. There are two small faces pressed up against the fence. They are giggling. "Look at his pee-pee," a small voice says. Jim turns away. They have ruined his moment. Is a man not free to do as he pleases in his own home, he wonders, to wash his own dirt from his body? Does he need permission? This is not America as Abe Lincoln intended.

He is angry and ashamed. He has the urge to turn the hose on the children but knows it will only start trouble. Instead, he moves cautiously, rinsing himself with his back to them and then wrapping the towel tightly around his waist. Jim carefully collects his clothing, the soap, and the hose, leaving no traces, and walks back towards the house, clean feet squeaking on the grass.

He sits in a straight-back chair in the living room, wet hair slicked back. Susan has bought all new furniture. Nothing is familiar. Nothing is comfortable. Jim goes into the kitchen and tries to make phone calls. His book is in his briefcase at the office. He can't think of where anyone lives and so can't get their numbers from information. He sits in his chair, in the dark, until his wife and children return. They have stopped at McDonald's on their way home; he can smell it on their clothing.

He takes the sleeping Emily, his little french fry, from Susan and carries her up to bed.

"Why were you home this afternoon?" Susan asks when he comes downstairs.

He points up towards Emily's bedroom and motions for Susan to whisper. "Bomb threat," he says.

"Nobody else came home early?" Susan says as if she doesn't believe him.

"It wasn't the whole city, just my building, my firm to be exact."

"How odd," she says. "Will you go in tomorrow?"

It has not occurred to Jim that he might not be going to the office in the morning. Susan goes upstairs to remind Jake to put his retainer in. The phone rings and Jim picks it up, hoping it will be someone from work.

"Is Susan there?" a male voice asks.

"No, I'm sorry, she's not."

"This is Bob Wellington. I ran into her at the car place the other day and I just wanted to make sure she got her tires rotated all right."

"They seem very well rotated," Jim says.

"How many miles you got on that car?"

"I wouldn't know," Jim says.

"Well, remind her to check on the oil change: every thirty-five hundred miles, even though they say you can wait to four or five. Runs the engine down if you wait, kills the car."

"I'll pass the information on."

"Is this her father by chance?" Bob Wellington asks, chuckling.

"No, it's not," Jim says.

"Well, good talking to you," Bob says.

"People must think you're divorced," Jim says to Susan, as they undress and get ready for bed. He sees her taking off her slip and underwear and imagines that Susan has secretly gotten a job on her own. She is a suburban callgirl, saving tips to buy a house at the beach. If she works hard enough, she could have a house in the Hamptons by next summer.

"You're at the office a lot," she says.

"What about these other guys, don't they have to work?"

Susan goes downstairs. Jim follows her. She tries to start the dishwasher. It runs for a second, makes a horrible sound, then stops.

"Damn," she says.

"Here, let me try." He goes over to the dishwasher, opens the door, closes the door, pushes the start button again, and looks down at the machine. Nothing happens.

"I'll call Robbie Martin," Susan says.

"You don't have to call anybody," Jim says.

"You certainly can't fix it. You have no idea of what to do."

It is true Jim doesn't know what to do with anything. Somehow he is content to leave it all alone and assume that it will heal itself.

Jim returns to the bedroom, takes off his pajamas, and dresses again.

"Where are you going?" Susan asks when she sees him dressed and heading for the door.

"Nowhere."

He starts the car and pulls it up close to the house, aiming the lights towards the yard. He flicks on the high beams and gets out. Jim re-plants the marigolds, constantly looking over his shoulder fearful that a band of sixteen-year-olds will mistake the lights for a party. He imagines they will find him, think he is an old man, bind and gag him, then go into his house, turn on the stereo, and eat everything, including his wife and children.

The telephone rings at quarter to six in the morning and Jim immediately thinks of death.

"Hello," he says, waiting for the bad news.

"Mr. Train," his secretary says, "Mr. Patterson's secretary called me and asked me to tell you we won't be opening the office today. The police are still investigating."

"Thanks for letting me know," Train says. "You wouldn't happen to have Howe or Worth's numbers, would you?"

"I'll get them and call back."

"No hurry," Train says, hanging up and falling back into a pleasant, productive dream about redesigning the office so that it seems more like a home, with soft couches and televisions; the kind of place where a man could live as well as work.

At seven-thirty Susan gets up. Jim lies in bed and watches her dress.

"Aren't you feeling well?" Susan asks.

"Fine," he says, pulling the blanket up to his chin.

Susan puts on her makeup before her blouse and then makes a big show of getting her blouse over her head without it touching her makeup. Jim is tempted to suggest it would be easier to do it in the reverse, but says nothing. In the mirror Susan's face is pulled down like she's had a stroke, and she's adding more mascara to her eyes, so that her lashes look like licorice sticks.

"Why don't you get up," she says. "You can drive Jake to school."

The last time Jim drove him to school, Jake spent the whole ride insulting his father. "You're going the wrong way," he yelled. "Don't you even know where my school is? You missed the short cut." Jim stopped the car at the top of a hill, got out, and walked around to the other side.

"You drive," Jim said.

"Dad," his son whined. "Dad, get back in the car. You're making me late."

Jake sounded exactly like Susan. Jim stood there in the street waiting for the boy to say, You're acting like a child. After ten minutes of absolute silence, Jim got back in and drove the rest of the way to Jake's school.

"Are you going to drive him?" Susan asks, putting the finishing touches on her exterior with a sea sponge.

"He can walk," Jim says.

He lies in bed waiting for his secretary to call back. Susan goes downstairs to get the children ready for school and then, without saying good-bye, she leaves with them.

Jim thinks of Patterson's plant and wonders whose plant he'll pee in years from now. He imagines sneaking into the associates' offices after they've left and letting go a little bit in each office, in every corner, revenge against the uncommitted, the false promise of youth and ambition. He sees himself convinced it is his secret, when in reality everyone will know. They'll give new guys cans of air freshener to keep hidden in their desks. New plants will be delivered weekly. No one will dare say anything to

Jim because, after all, he is Train, the Train of Flynch, Peabody, Patterson, and Train.

At nine his secretary calls with Howe's number.

"Worth is seriously unlisted."

Jim writes the number on the back of a magazine and tells her to have a good day.

"I will," she says. "There's a sale at Macy's."

He lifts himself out of bed tenderly as though just returned from a hernia operation. He takes the steps slowly, as if in pain. How can he be in the house, mid-morning, mid-week, except as a sick person?

Jim calls Howe. The number rings ten times before Howe picks up the phone. Jim stands in the kitchen, the phone tucked under his chin, his free hands randomly plucking bits of food out of the refrigerator and popping them into his mouth.

"What took you so long?" Jim asks.

"I thought my wife was going to get it. It's usually for her."

"Any news?" Jim asks.

"My wife is kicking me out of the house. She says I can't come back until six o'clock, preferably seven. I'm driving her crazy."

Jim lets the refrigerator door close, and rinses off his fingers in the sink.

"I guess I'll go and buy some shoes, shirts, stuff for the office," Howe says.

"Big sale at Macy's," Jim says.

"Then that's where I'll be. Any details about the bomb?"

"Nothing," Jim says. "You?"

"Last I heard they were still checking. Kind of weird, isn't it?"

"It is and it isn't," Jim says.

He thinks of himself as the closest thing the firm has to an in-house philosopher.

"Yeah, guess so," Howe says. "Well, the housekeeper wants to use the phone. I better let her."

Jim's call-waiting beeps.

"See you," Jim says, pressing down the receiver button. "Hello?"

"Is this Bill's Repair Man?" a woman's voice asks.

"No, it's not," Jim says. "He was here yesterday."

"This is Jill Robinson. Leave a message for Mrs. Train that I'll meet her at the Chew-Chew, in town, at one?"

A loud noise in the basement/garage startles Jim. He hangs up without saying anything, grabs a butcher knife, and runs downstairs.

"Don't move," he yells at the man stealing his lawn-mower.

"Who are you?" the man asks.

"The question is who are you?" Jim says, waving the knife around.

"I come to cut the grass, but I don't need this shit," the man says, dropping the mower bag and walking out of the garage to his truck parked in the driveway.

Jim is in the process of reorganizing the cutlery drawer when Susan comes in at noon.

"Why aren't you dressed?" she asks.

"I have nothing to do," Jim says, sadly.

Jim is not himself. Without his work, he is a dark and depressed man.

"Get dressed. We'll have lunch in town," Susan says.

"You're meeting Jill Robinson at the Chew-Chew at one."

"Then hurry," Susan says.

"Well, hello," Jill says in a voice that's a little too friendly.

It's the first time they've met. Without asking, Jim knows she's a real estate broker—that's what women around here are if they're not social workers, or in rare cases pediatricians. Jill is too hyperactive to be a social worker, too stupid to be a doctor. If Susan weren't there, he'd sit Jill down at the bar and discuss the possibilities of selling his house, or burning it to get the insurance money.

"Is everything all right? You can tell me, I can keep a secret," Jill says.

For how long, Jim wonders, five minutes?

Jill is clearly excited. The only time she's ever seen a husband following his wife around on a weekday is when one of them has just been diagnosed with something horrible, like infertility or breast cancer.

"Did you have a doctor's appointment this morning?" Jill asks.

"No," Susan says. "A bomb threat."

Jill's eyes light up. The waitress asks if anyone would like a drink and Jim thinks of having a martini but doesn't because there's something about the way Jill's looking at him that makes him sure she'd tell everyone he was an alcoholic.

"B.L.T. and a Coke," Jim says.

Susan and Jill talk about houses: what's good, bad, broken, and who fixes it. Clearly this is where Bill's Repair Man came from.

Jill's been inside every house in the area and keeps a running score of who has what in terms of cars, large-screen televisions, walk-in freezers, etc. Jim thinks if she could keep her mouth shut, she'd make a killing as a burglar.

When he can't stand it any longer, he excuses himself

from the table by saying he has to make a phone call—
"Checking in with the office," he says. Jim goes to the bar
and orders a double martini, careful to keep his head low.
Through the potted plants he watches Susan and Jill, wondering what Susan sees in Jill—it's not like her to be
friends with a woman who frosts her hair. Perhaps she's
changing, he thinks—as though this sort of a change is a
precursor to something more serious, like Alzheimer's.

He tosses back the martini and returns to the table, face
flushed, just as the waitress is putting the lunch plates
down. Jim picks at his sandwich carefully, knowing if a
leaf of lettuce or a piece of bacon were to lodge in his
throat he would be unable or unwilling to free it, and in all
likelihood neither would Susan.

He pictures himself choking, looking at Susan and Jill as
the world around him gets smaller.

"Should we do something?" Jill will ask—she can never
do anything without asking someone's opinion first.

"No," Susan will say, "let him go. It's all right."

He imagines himself falling to the floor, Susan and Jill
looking at him sweetly for a moment, like he's a child
imitating a dog. As his eyes roll back in his head, the
women return to their conversation, and the last thing
Jim hears has something to do with winterizing.

This is not a solution, he tells himself, ending the choking scenario. This is not the way to go. At the office, at the
office, he thinks, sucking on his thoughts like they're loz-
enges, I'd be talking to my secretary who likes me very
much, having a drink in the restaurant next door, buying
snacks from the blind man in the lobby, looking out the
window, watering Patterson's plant. His eyes water. He
almost cries. Everything is okey-dokey, he tells himself.
It's going to be all right.

"Aren't you well?" Jill asks Jim.

She is used to men who shovel food into their mouths

without looking up until finally, when there is no more, they lift their eyes and burp simultaneously.

"Fine, thank you," Jim says.

"Finished?" the waitress asks as she clears the plates.

"Thank you," Jim says, plucking the colored plastic swords from his sandwich before she takes the plate.

"How cute," Jill says.

"Do you want to come with us to the mall?" Susan asks Jim, waving her eyebrows up and down, as though she's making a special offer.

"I think I'll just walk home," he says, standing up. "It's a nice day for a walk. Good meeting you." He pumps Jill's hand as though the up-and-down action turns the key to a spring that winds him up so he can toddle home.

It is a beautiful day, the most beautiful day Jim can ever remember seeing. The sky is brilliant blue, the trees are full of leaves, there's a light breeze. It's perfect except the streets are deserted, there are no people, no babysitters, no strollers, nothing. The stillness makes Jim uncomfortable. He feels as though something horrible has happened and everyone except him knew enough to run away. When he turns the next corner, a giant mutant killer will be waiting for him. It will reach down from above the trees and he will never know what hit him. He walks quickly, sure that he will die before he reaches home. He can feel it in his chest. If nothing reaches down to snatch him, it will happen anyway. He will collapse. He will lie crumpled on the sidewalk. The cars driving past him will not see Jim in the suit, they will see only the suit, and think it is a heap of clothing left out for charity to collect. He begins to run. He runs faster and faster until he sees the spastic boy standing in his regular place. The sight of the boy calms him and Jim stops running and begins waving from very far away. The boy waves back.

"I'm home early," he says as soon as he's close enough to talk.

"Did you lose your job?" the boy groans in a voice that is as twisted as his body.

Jim shakes his head. "No."

"That's good, I'm happy," the boy says and waves goodbye.

As Jim goes up the steps to the house he thinks about work. If they cancel it again tomorrow he will go in anyway. He will simply arrive at the office. If the guards won't let him upstairs, he will refuse to go home; he will throw himself on their mercy.

THE BULLET CATCHER

Frank hovered near the frost-free refrigerators listening to a conversation two aisles over.

"Gross, Julie, what are we getting here—pull-on pants? A washer-dryer? It's not going to fit into the bag."

"Open the other one, it's emptier."

"You know I'm not supposed to shoplift anymore."

"Don't take that, idiot! It has a sensor."

He worked his way into power tools hoping that between chain saws he'd see them. At the end of the row he poked his head around the corner. There were three girls with what he and his wife called big hair. One of them slowly turned around and dropped a blender into her shopping bag. It was Julie, his neighbors' daughter, his Saturday-evening babysitter.

"Gross, a blender. What do you need that for?"

"I can make diet drinks in my room. Besides, eventually Christmas will come and I'll need presents," Julie said.

"A blender is good. No one would ever steal a blender," the other girl said. Except for fingernails a mile long, red like they'd been dipped in fresh blood, she had no distinguishing features.

Julie put a mini-chopper in on top of the blender.

"Hurry up, I'm hungry," the third girl said. She had big

breasts and wore a very short T-shirt that barely covered them, and no bra. Frank wondered if anyone had suggested that perhaps it was time she restrain herself.

"How could you be hungry? You just ate a cheeseburger and fries."

Her breasts were growing, Frank thought, they needed food.

"I threw it up."

"Are you serious?" the girl with the nails asked.

The overdeveloped girl nodded. He decided to call her Tina.

"Is this, like, a problem?" Julie asked.

"I just need a frozen yogurt or something. I have a really bad taste in my mouth," Tina said.

"I'm sure," Nails said.

Nails put a blow dryer in on top of everything and they walked out of the store.

Frank hung back as the girls got closer to the entrance. He didn't want to be right there when the security guards grabbed them. He waited by a rack of large-size flower print dresses and watched the girls walk untouched into the body of the mall. Then he hurried to catch up, wondering if it was his obligation to stop them, to drag them kicking, screaming, swearing, maybe even yelling rape, to the manager's office.

He checked his watch. He was supposed to be buying tires. He was supposed to meet his wife at the Twistie Freeze at the other end of the mall in twenty minutes.

"Oh my God, turn around, walk the other way," Nails said.

"Why?" Tina asked.

"Get with the program. It's Adam."

"So?"

"Is your bulb, like, only sixty watts?

"Oh, Adam," Nails screamed down the mall. A boy

standing in front of the record store—which, Frank noticed, didn't sell records anymore, only tapes and CDs—tensed. "Adam, look who's here." Nails pointed her finger like a gun at Julie's ear. "It's Julie."

Julie slapped Nails' hand down. Nails dropped her shopping bag and slapped Julie back.

"Bitch, I was trying to help you!" she said.

In the middle of the mall Nails and Julie clawed at each other with fingernails like switchblades.

"Come here," Nails said to Adam.

As he moved to come towards them, he stepped on his shoelaces—intentionally untied, as was the style—and fell forward, catching himself in a position similar to the peak of a push-up.

Frank felt the fall in his stomach, the horrible sensation of failure, the tripping of mankind.

Adam lay face-down on the floor as though his embarrassment was enough to kill him.

The girls laughed and walked away, their claws magically retracted by the punch line of Adam's fall.

In McDonald's, Frank stood in line next to the girls and when he and Julie accidently made eye contact, he blushed the same shade of red she did.

"Hi," he said.

"Yeah." She immediately looked down at the floor.

Frank looked at her and wondered about what she did alone in his house, with his children, on Saturday nights. He came up with nothing specific but in general the thought frightened him.

Sitting in a molded plastic booth that reminded him of his daughter's play furniture, he tried to spy on the girls. A tropical plant blocked his view. He ate a few fries and sipped the Coke. The girls were silent. Frank started to think he smelled something burning. He lifted one of the french fries to his nose and sniffed it. He extended his neck and inhaled, testing the air around him . . . plastic burning.

The three girls were kleptomaniacs, pyromaniacs, probably nymphomaniacs as well. He closed his eyes, conjuring an image of himself with a fifteen-year-old girl in a scenario that involved giggling, posing, uncoordinated and inappropriate body movements, and frustration that ultimately resulted in a spanking that was definitely pleasurable, at least for him.

A second wave of the odor overcame him. They were probably flicking their Bics against the Styrofoam containers their burgers and nuggets came in, melting them into cute little animal shapes or costume jewelry, like an arts-and-crafts project. They were burning everything. Next they'd try out the tropical plant. *Is it real, Julie? I don't know, light it. Real things don't burn.* He imagined McDonald's on fire, melting. He saw himself trying to escape, stuck in a hot pool of liquid plastic like a mouse in a glue trap. He smelled matches but no cigarettes. He smelled plastic burning and thought of toxic fumes filling the mall, working like nerve gas, killing thousands of people who would never know what hit them, the credit cards in their wallets forever fusing with their flesh.

Frank jumped up, jutting his tray out in front of him, brandishing it like a weapon. The girls were way ahead, on their way out. He glanced at their table; they'd left their trash. He went towards it; the Styrofoam containers were singed, but only slightly. There were at least twenty-five burnt matches dunked in a pool of ketchup. He sifted through the garbage—picked up a half-eaten burger and took two bites before he realized what he was doing and put it down. Under everything he found "Adam and Julie 2 Gather 4 Ever" burned into the Formica tabletop. It was still warm.

"You spelled it wrong," Frank started to shout. The

word *You* came out in a loud passionate voice before he realized it was pointless. Spelling meant nothing to the girls. Frank went towards the exit, tray still very much in hand. A McDonald's security guard stopped him.

"Sorry, sir, you'll have to consume that in here."

Frank tried to peak around the guard. He shifted to one side and poked his head out. The guard shifted with him and blocked his view.

"Your fries are getting cold," the guard said.

Frank dumped his tray into a trash can, and raced into the center of the mall. Walking briskly, almost running, he went down the center of what felt like a nightmare; a brightly lit fluorescent tube filled with seating groups and planters set up like obstacles. He went after the girls asking himself, What am I chasing? What am I doing?

He went through the mall, weaving in and out of people, strollers, breathing hard, looking for Julie, Nails, and Tina, their big hair, their mini-skirts, their overloaded shopping bags. Instead of seeing them or seeing nothing at all, he saw hundreds of girls just like them, identical twins. Like in a mirror ball, a million reflections spun across the mall. High hair, skinny legs, faces caked with makeup like in a science fiction movie. They were everywhere, as though it were a dream. A strange and disturbing element came upon him like a hidden danger, causing him to panic. Boys. Suddenly, he was aware of an almost equal number of boys in dark T-shirts with bloody daggers decaled onto the front, roaming freely. They were thick in the neck, arm, and thigh, and walked slightly off balance, an overbred species. Male and female, hanging out as if this were some private party in someone's living room. The mating game. They pressed into corners, leaned back against pay phones, and exchanged phone numbers and deep kisses. They lay on the floor in front of their favorite stores, stretched out, heads propped on elbows, watching the people go by like they were watching something on MTV.

A security guard, who could have passed for a twelve-year-old dressed up for Halloween, walked by Frank. He smiled at the girls and rested his hands on the heavy leather equipment belt around his waist. The girls blushed. Frank imagined the boys took turns playing cop. When they got to the mall they flipped for it and then the winner (or was it the loser?) changed into the uniform. Frank noticed the guard had a gun, a real gun, and wondered why a twelve-year-old in a Halloween costume was carrying a real gun.

His watch beeped. He had set the alarm for the time he was supposed to meet his wife in front of the Twistie Freeze. Visually, he made another quick sweep of the area and then walked towards a clump of what looked like airport lounge chairs near the Twistie Freeze.

He sat there for a minute before he was overcome by self-consciousness and had to get up again. He went into the Twistie Freeze, bought a vanilla-and-chocolate-twist cone, and stood licking it near the door.

Across the mall, a baseball team was having a party in the Cheezy Dog. When Frank was a kid they always had barbecues after their games. They'd stay in the park playing catch and stuffing their faces until one kid threw up and then they'd all climb into someone's father's station wagon and be dropped off one by one in the sadness of dark.

Frank looked in the Cheezy Dog and saw some kid take his hot dog out of the roll, hold it in front of his crotch, and wag it at the waitress. He quickly looked away.

At the far end of the mall, a shiny jeep was parked in the middle of things. At first Frank thought it made no sense, but as he thought about it more he became convinced it was the perfect idea; he couldn't believe someone hadn't thought of it before. A car dealership in a mall. Perfecto! It was the one way to get men to come back again and again, to spend hours, lingering.

Frank stood in front of the jeep, dreaming of a different kind of life, the kind he'd read about in stories of men outdoors, fishing trips and cabins in the woods. He dripped a bit of frozen custard onto the jeep and blotted it off with his napkin, leaving a smeary place on the hood. He fantasized buying a second home somewhere by a lake.

The jeep was wrapped in plastic tape that looked like the stuff police use to rope off crime scenes. It had Z-100 printed all over it.

"What's Z-100?" he asked a kid standing next to him.

"Great metal station," the kid said.

It was as if the child had spoken in code. What the hell was a metal station, Frank wanted to know.

"What's Z-100?" he asked again.

"A radio station. They're giving it away, in about fifteen minutes," an older woman said.

He walked in circles around the jeep. He checked the sticker: fourteen thousand six hundred bucks; AM/FM radio, cassette deck, rustproof, good tires, mud flaps. He finished his cone and planned a new life. As he ran over the figures in his head and realized that any life other than the one he already lived was a complete impossibility, he became furious. Who were all the people in the mall, carrying around big shopping bags full of who knows what? They couldn't all be shoplifters. They were buying things, big, important things. Where did they get the money? They couldn't all be millionaires.

A crowd formed around Frank and the car. People started setting up folding beach chairs and plastic coolers, like what you'd put in the backyard or by the pool, in a ring around the car. The contest hadn't even started yet, and already a bottle of two hundred and fifty aspirins had been opened and was lying next to a can of Diet Coke.

The contest, I want to be in the contest, Frank thought. He imagined how proud Mary and the kids would be if he actually won something, especially something large like a car.

"Sign me up," he said to someone wearing a judge's hat.

"What's your name?"

"Frank Mann."

She looked down at her list. "Your name's not here."

"But I want to be in the contest," he whined like a child.

"Did you call in and win?"

Frank gave her a confused look.

"The first twenty people who were the one-hundredth callers when we played the Poizon Boiz 'Roll My Wheels' are in the contest. Obviously you're not one."

"There has to be some way."

"Sorry," the judge said, walking away.

Frank continued to accost anyone in a Z-100 T-shirt until another judge pulled him aside and explained in extreme detail how the entrants had qualified. There was no way to sign up late.

Frank was so upset it was all he could do to contain a tantrum. He pictured himself screaming and pointing and calling everyone names until the security force, the boy with the gun, came for him, and like a civil disobedient he went limp and had to be dragged from the mall.

"Sore loser," some girl with very big hair would say as they swept him past her.

Frank saw Julie on the other side of the car, sitting in one of the lounge chairs. He worked his way over to her.

"Are you a winner?"

"Yeah, but I had to pretend I was my mother. You have to be twenty-one to get the car. She's doing the contest."

Julie pointed at her mother, who was in a huddle with the other contestants and the judges from the radio station.

"How's it work?" Frank asked.

"You have to keep your hands on the car all the time, except five minutes an hour. No other part of your body can ever touch the car, and like, if you want, someone can stay here with you overnight."

Without thinking Frank offered to stay overnight. He imagined himself prowling the corridors at 3 A.M.

"That's okay," Julie said. "I'm staying."

A short ugly man with permanent acne began speaking into a megaphone. His voice was like chocolate mousse, deep and smooth; he was obviously a disc jockey. The contestants arranged themselves around the car, scurrying for what they thought was the best place, the hood versus the side, and so on.

"Are your hands ready?" the D.J. asked.

The contestants and Frank nodded.

"Put your paws on the car."

The contestants seemed to surge forward as the contest began, rocking the jeep slightly, perhaps raising it off the ground a half-inch or so before they settled into the poses they would have to hold for the next fifty-five minutes.

Within five minutes most of the crowd dissipated. As far as they were concerned there was nothing to look at.

By the time Mary showed up at the Twistee Freeze forty-five minutes late, Frank was morbidly depressed, filled with a second ice cream cone and a complete hatred for the American way.

"All done?" Mary asked.

"I didn't get to the tires yet," he said.

"Another time."

"Maybe tomorrow," Frank said.

She handed him her packages to carry and they walked

back towards where they had originally come from.

They passed Julie's friends, standing outside the record store smoking. Mary stopped. "You shouldn't be smoking," she said.

Frank stood behind her feeling incredibly bloated: part of a large Coke, half an order of fries, a couple of bites of one of the girls' burger, and two ice cream cones. He stood in back of Mary, his stomach jutting out in front of him, not believing that he'd let himself get to this point.

Behind Mary's back, he lifted a finger to his ear and spun it in circles. Nails and Tina didn't respond. He did the bit where he took a make-believe grenade out of his pocket, pulled the pin, threw it, plugged his ears, and ducked his head to escape the explosion. Still nothing.

The two girls stood there staring, listening to Mary as though they were used to listening but never taking anything in.

Frank didn't resist when Mary reached behind her, took his hand, and led him away.

"I'll have to come back tomorrow," he told Mary, twisting his head around to see if they were laughing at him.

"I have a meeting. I won't be able to come with you," she said as though there were some rule about Frank going to the mall alone.

"So?"

"Sew buttons," she said.

It was what she always said when there was nothing left to say.

The next evening he waited until Mary left for her meeting, then said good-bye to the kids and took off for the mall. He drove fast, imagining that if he didn't get there soon, he would begin to shrivel like a helium balloon, slowly dropping down, sinking lower and lower, until he hovered six inches above the floor. By morning he'd be airless, dead, on the bucket seats.

The Pyramid Mall floated in a sea of parking spaces, laid out thirty deep so that on any given day or evening, with the exception of Saturdays, a person could find a place within ten spaces of the end and enter the mall feeling somehow lucky. The only thing pyramid-like about the place were pyramid-shaped planters filled with half-dead geraniums.

He pulled into a good space near Sears feeling what he called the guilt of necessary purpose. He had come here for a real reason. Tires. Before he could do anything, he had to go directly into Sears. He had to accomplish something so that later he could tell Mary how wonderful he was.

There were no salespeople in the tire department and Frank was too distracted to hunt one down. Frank had a certain pale nonexistence to him, like Casper the Ghost. He could fight it if he wanted to. He could summon his energy and make himself a kind of lifelike pinkish-purple that could get a fair amount of attention, but he couldn't sustain it. In Sears, he couldn't even bring himself up to a kind of light flesh tone. He just didn't have it in him. He took heart in knowing it was highly unlikely he'd ever be taken hostage in a bank robbery or hijacking.

He left Sears promising himself he'd deal with the tires later; if necessary he'd go directly to a tire store where salesmen waited day and night for guys like Frank to walk in. He went into the mall charged by the prospect of a new project—an unexpected surprise, like a bonus—finding something to buy, to bring home to Mary like show and tell.

Just outside Sears, two women from the local Red Cross

sat at a folding table with a blood pressure cuff between them waiting for a victim. The atmosphere was festive. Diet experts in workout clothing mingled freely. *Stop Smoking Now.* Lungs like giant latex condoms expanded and collapsed. *Mental Illness: The Hidden Symptoms.* He reviewed the list without intending to. Bad news. According to Frank's own evaluation he had all the signs of Chronic Untreated Disturbance. According to the description he was a time bomb that could go at any minute. No warning. Health Fair '90 ended in front of Woolworth's. Two candy-striped cardboard poles marked the beginning and the end.

Frank spotted Adam—the kid who tripped over his laces the day before—in the record store. He went directly to him and slapped his hand down on the counter, stinging his palm.

"Hey, Adam," Frank said.

Adam was startled. He looked down at his shirt to see if he was wearing a name tag. He wasn't.

"Adam, talk to me."

"What?"

"Tell me about CDs—are there different kinds? Different sizes? Do they all play on the same machine?"

For the past two years, everything Frank saw or read nagged him about CDs.

Adam looked at Frank like Frank was an extraterrestrial, an undercover cop, or some new brand of idiot. He didn't say anything. The silence made Frank uncomfortable. He wanted to be friends.

"I'm serious, Adam. I'm very serious."

Adam kept staring, checking out Frank. He wanted to be sure he didn't end up on the wrong end of a joke.

"They're all the same," Adam finally said, tentatively. "You get a player and plug it into your stereo, or you can get a portable."

"What do you have?"

"Portable. I plug it into my car stereo. That's really cool."

"I bet."

Adam looked at Frank like he was still waiting for something to happen. Maybe Frank was someone's father coming to tell Adam he didn't want his daughter riding around in Adam's car with Adam blasting her eardrums anymore.

"What do you listen to?"

"I dunno," Adam said, suddenly shy.

"Well, what do your friends listen to?"

"All kinds of stuff."

"If I wanted to buy something, what would you recommend?"

"New Poizon Boiz just came in," Adam said happily.

"I'll take one. Do you sell the players here?" he asked, handing Adam his American Express card.

"You get them at Wire Wizard, upstairs, just across from King Pin."

As Adam was ringing Frank up, a big-haired girl, identical to Julie, Tina, and Nails, came up to Adam, wrapped her arms around his neck, and pushed her tongue down Adam's throat.

Every organ in Frank's body jumped. His insides rose up. He signed the charge slip, turned around, and went straight to the Wire Wizard.

"I need a CD player," he said desperately to the salesman.

"What kind?"

"A good one. A very good one. I have to be able to plug it into my stereo or my car." He felt flushed and out of breath. He thought of the freshness of a fifteen-year-old body.

"We have a few like that."

"I want the best. I have to have the best," Frank said, excitedly.

"The best is not necessarily the most expensive."

"I know that," Frank said.

What kind of guy did this kid take him for? He tapped his fingers on the counter.

"Give me what you've got," Frank said to the guy.

He felt like he had to hurry. He had to finish this soon. He had to go back and see what Adam was doing.

"This is a very good model," the guy said, taking something out of the case.

"Great," Frank said, without looking at the player. He laid his charge card on the counter, sure that this was how people did it. Credit was free, easy, there was always someone giving it away, asking you to take more.

"Do you want to hear it?"

"I trust you. I really do," Frank said, looking the guy in the eye for half a second.

When Frank got out of the Wire Wizard, Adam was gone. Lunch break, his manager said, winking.

On the down escalator Frank pulled the receipt out of the Wire Wizard bag. A hundred and eighty-nine dollars. He couldn't believe it. He'd figured it would cost fifty or sixty bucks, seventy-five at most. What had he done? What would Mary say? He quickly shifted his attitude to a more adaptive one. I'm allowed. I am absolutely allowed. I deserve it. He wouldn't tell Mary. He would find something else to bring home, something smaller, perhaps something specifically for her, like a present.

From the escalator he saw the crowd around the jeep. He counted the number of contestants left. Since yesterday eleven had walked away. According to the woman on the escalator in front of Frank, they'd thrown up their hands and asked to be let out. One had to be taken by ambulance when, for no apparent reason, she started vomiting.

"How're you doing?" he asked Julie's mother.

She smiled and nodded her head.

"It's nothing yet," Julie's mother said. "Tomorrow it'll start getting good."

"I'll be here," Frank said.

"So will I."

Frank felt his presence did something to the contest. He had the idea that the way he looked at the contestants either gave them what they needed to go on or broke them right there on the spot. He felt powerful and necessary.

They were down to nine. They all looked willing to call it a day. An incredible assortment of junk food was scattered half-eaten among the lounge chairs and coolers; fast food from every carry-out in the mall had been supplemented by special-request items like Ding-Dongs and cream soda. It surprised Frank that no one thought of the nutrition edge. No one seemed to think eating right during the five-minute breaks might make all the difference. There were no Tiger's Milk bars, no bowls of pasta salad, not even any goddamn Gatorade. Who were these people? Frank wanted to know. He really wanted to know. He imagined interviewing them during their breaks, like Geraldo Rivera, asking what it felt like to touch the car, why they chose to spend their break standing, talking on a pay phone, instead of lying down? He wanted to know why no one was wearing support stockings or using heating pads on long extension cords.

As he stood trying to figure out how he could become an official consultant, a girl right in front of him was disqualified. Her knee buckled and her hip banged against the car.

"You're out," the judge called like an umpire in a base-ball game.

With a completely bewildered look on her face she stepped away from the car. Frank saw the sweaty prints her hands left on the hood. Instead of looking at the girl he looked at the other contestants. They were taking inventory, checking each other out, placing unspoken bets on the order in which they would fall.

Frank stayed until the mall closed. Store lights blinked on and off, warning customers that the end was coming soon. Assistant managers started pulling metal security gates down and fiddling with their keys. Frank thought of people left overnight, locked in. He started walking back in the direction of Sears and then turned around and took a last look at the contestants. He imagined them all changing into their pajamas during the eleven o'clock break. Frank silently said good night to the remaining eight players and barely made it through Sears before they locked the doors. He had nothing for Mary.

On the way home he stopped at the all-night Super Pharmacy and bought Mary a Dustbuster. As he pulled into the driveway, he stuffed the bags from the Wire Wizard and the record store under the car seat.

That night, waiting to fall asleep, Frank thought of contests he'd seen on the evening news. National coverage for three people out there somewhere, sitting on a billboard scaffold. His heart swelled. The Pyramid Mall was his own, he'd been there from the start. No matter who eventually drove away with the car, part of it belonged to Frank.

The next day, he fought the urge to call the mall from his office, a cubbyhole in an overdeveloped industrial park, and ask for an update. After work, when all the accounts were reconciled, he hurried home and found his neighbor, Julie's father, sitting at his dining room table, waiting for dinner.

"My whole damn family's living out there at the mall," he said between chicken legs.

Frank didn't answer. He waited until Julie's father went home and then told Mary he was leaving.

"I have to go see about those tires," he said to Mary.

"I thought you did that last night?"

"Didn't get what I needed. I have to go back and get it over with."

On his way to the contest, he stopped by the sporting goods store. He slipped a baseball glove on and pounded his fist into the mitt a couple of times. It could heal him, he thought. It could be just the thing. With the exception of what he'd seen two days ago at the Cheezy Dog, the mitt reminded him of the better things in life. He used to have a mitt until his son had taken it to school one day and lost it.

With his free hand Frank started pulling bats out of the rack, turning them over and over, awkwardly tossing them slightly into the air, spinning and catching them, bending and flexing the glove on his left hand.

The glove was fifty-six dollars. He couldn't do it. He'd already done it last night. There was no way. He took it off and put it tenderly down on the pile, hiding it near the back, leaving room for his dreams.

In the middle of the mall, in the center of what he had come to think of as the runway, he saw Nails and Tina. Frank kept his shoulders pulled back and reminded himself that he was a grown-up and they were children. Tina stood in front of him, licking her ice cream cone in an intentionally obscene way.

"Oh, hi," she said, pretending to all of a sudden see him.

He almost died. There were men his age who had heart attacks and called it a day over less.

"Well, gotta go," Tina finally said, her cone completely gone, a ring of chocolate outlining her lips like liner.

Sixty-seven hours into the contest. Frank promised himself that when this was over everything would be better. It already was better, he told himself.

Julie's mom and a guy ten years younger were the only contestants left. The guy wore a T-shirt his girlfriend had made for him that said *Get Your Hands Off My Car.*

Julie's mother had her shoes off, her knee-high stockings rolled down to her ankles. The ankles, purple and puffy, bulged out over the hose. She kept shifting her weight from side to side, foot to foot. She seemed more like a feral raccoon than most feral raccoons ever did. Her skin was pasty, her eyes had sunk deep into her head. The black around her eyes was heavy like someone had drawn it there with a charcoal briquet.

Enough! Frank wanted to yell. Stop. Give her the car, she's earned it.

Between twenty and thirty people stood in a circle around Julie's mom and the guy, looking at them as though they were objects on view, specimens from *Night of the Living Dead,* perfect examples of the devastating side effects of spending too much time indoors.

The scene was going sour for Frank. There was a definite spin to it, a dangerous whirling that could suck a person down, like a garbage disposal. There was too much to hear, and see, and eat. Frank decided that's why the kids were lying on the floor like cancerous lumps.

It couldn't last much longer. There was no way.

Frank looked at the last two contestants and then had to look away. They were pathetic, doughy, offering themselves up for human consumption like some ritualistic sacrifice. When looking away was not enough he had to walk away. He turned around and was going home when he heard a thick popping sound, like one a plunger makes when it comes up. He turned back towards the car. The thick sucking sound was Julie's mother's hands coming up off the hood. Her hands were rising up into the air, lifting over her head, but she was still shifting her weight from foot to foot and looking down at the car as though her hands were there.

"Mom, your hands, your hands!" Julie screamed.

The other contestant froze, his hands pressed so hard on the hood they made a dent.

When the judges got to Julie's mom, they reached up and pulled her hands down to her sides. Her arms fell like levers whose springs had snapped.

She looked up and said, "What?"

Julie ran over and started shaking her. "Mom, you idiot, you lost the contest. You lost when we were so close to winning."

Frank hated Julie. She was unbelievable. A hateful child.

On the other side of the car, the guy with the T-shirt was being pounded on the back in a manner that was vaguely resuscitative, like CPR or the Heimlich maneuver.

A guy next to Frank had a radio tuned to Z-100.

"We have a winner at the Pyramid Mall," the D.J. said. "Let's go there live."

Over the radio, Frank heard the guy thanking his parents and his girlfriend. The weird thing was that Frank was looking right at the guy and the guy wasn't talking at all. He was just standing there staring. There were no microphones anywhere. Over the radio Frank heard all kinds of yelling and screaming and a round of "For He's a

Jolly Good Fellow," by "all John's friends." But at the mall, with the exception of Julie yelling at her mother, it was quiet.

One of the judges handed Julie's mom an envelope.

Frank asked someone who appeared to be in charge what it was.

"Second place. Two hundred and fifty dollars," he said.

"Two hundred and fifty dollars. That's all she gets?" Frank said. "He gets a car and all she gets is a lousy two hundred and fifty bucks. Unbelievable. You guys are unbelievable. She stood on her fucking feet for sixty-seven hours and forty-eight minutes and all you're giving her is nothing."

People stared at the ground while he talked.

He felt sick. He was sick. Vomit and rage and junk food rose in him. He looked at the girl from the radio station. She shrugged. With her shoulders up near her neck, shrugging, she looked certifiably retarded. In order to keep from hitting her, from holding her personally responsible, Frank ran. He ran down the length of the mall and back again. He did it three times before he ended up at the sporting goods store.

Frank ran into the sporting goods store, grabbed the glove he'd hidden, put it on his hand, raised his arm above his head, and screamed: "It's mine. It's mine. I'm taking it. It belongs to me."

When he got no response, he ran through the store, waving his arm and the glove, still screaming. He ran through the store, out the door, and down the middle of the mall. At some point he was aware someone was chasing him, but it meant nothing. He slammed through a set of fire doors, triggered an alarm, and ended up on the edge of the parking lot, at twilight. The earth and the sky were the same deep shade of blue.

"Stop," the kid dressed as a guard yelled, his voice

cracking. "Please stop where you are. Stop. Freeze."

Each time the guard shouted he was more insistent. Each time, Frank became more frenzied. He zigzagged unsteadily. He heard a shot ring through the air behind him.

"Freeze."

Frank was near the far edge of the lot, a tall hill of fill-dirt in front of him. He whirled around and crouched down, low, like a catcher. He raised the glove up in front of his face and caught the second bullet.

It struck him like a punch. He rocked back and forth, heel to toe, before falling onto his back, his knees raised in front of him like insect legs.

There was a buzzing in his ears, like a telephone constantly ringing.

Frank lay on his back in the parking lot. No shopping carts wheeled past his head. No one came near him. The glove stayed in place and the crowd over by the mall imagined him skewered, permanently sewn together like a cheap doll, his expression fixed, his hand permanently placed.

It seemed like forever before anyone heard sirens. Red and white flashing lights sucked up the twilight and made it seem much later than it was. A paramedic jumped out and pressed his fingers to Frank's jugular.

"He's alive," the medic shouted and the crowd moved forward.

"Does anybody know who it is?" the medic asked. "Anyone know his name?"

"He lives across the street from me," Julie said.

Frank fainted behind the glove. The squawking of the police radio woke him up.

"We got a bullet catcher here. Security guard hit him, when he was trying to get away with something."

I wasn't trying to get away with anything, Frank

thought, and then fell back into a fuzzy kind of sleep.

They slid a board under Frank. He felt pressure, intense pressure, as though his insides were being pushed up and out. He was being squeezed to death. Perhaps they were running him over with a steamroller, pushing him into the fresh asphalt at the edge of the lot.

He tried to remember where he'd parked the car. The CD player was still under the seat. He hoped no one would ever find it. Mary would be annoyed that he hadn't gotten the tires. Sew buttons.

The medics didn't touch his face or attempt to remove the glove. They were saving that for the doctors. By the time they tied everything in place with heavy gauze the sky had dropped deep into darkness. The mall had closed for the night. The crowd evaporated: one by one, in a great snake of a line, all the cars pulled out onto the highway. The medics dressed Frank up like a spring float and wheeled him around in a quiet parade on the empty parking lot.

YOURS TRULY

I'm hiding in the linen closet writing letters to myself. This is the place where no one knows I am, where I can think without thinking about what anyone else would think or at least it's quiet. I don't want to scare anyone, but things can't go on like this.

Until today I could still go into the living room and talk to my mother's Saturday morning Fat Club. I could say, "Hi, how are you. That's a very nice dress. Magenta's such a good color, it hides the hips. Nice shoes too. I would never have thought of bringing pink and green together like that." I could pretend to be okay, but that's part of the problem.

In here, pressed up against the towels, the sheets, the heating pad, it's clear that everything is not hunky-dory. I've got one of those Itty Bitty Book Lights and I'm making notes.

Today is Odessa's day. At any minute she might turn the knob and let the world, disguised as daylight, come flooding in. She might do that and never know what she's done. She'll open the door and her eyes will get wide. She'll look at me and say, "Lord." She'll say, "You could have given me a heart attack." And I'll think, Yes, I could have, but I'm having one myself and there isn't room for two in the same place at the same time. She'll look at my face and I'll have to look at the floor. She won't know that having someone look directly at me, having someone expect me to look at her, causes a sharp pain that begins in my eyes, ricochets off my skull, and in the end makes my entire skeleton shake. She won't know that I can't look at anything except the towels without being overcome with emotion. She won't know that at the sight of another person I weep, I wish to embrace and be embraced, and then to kill. She won't get that I'm dangerous.

Odessa will open the door and see me standing with this tiny light, clipped to the middle shelf, with the pad of paper on top of some extra blankets, with two extra pencils sticking out of the space between the bath sheets and the Turkish towels. She'll see all this and ask, "Are you all right?" I won't be able to answer. I can't tell her why I'm standing in a closet filled with enough towels to take a small town to the beach. I won't say, I'm not all right. God help me, I'm not. I will simply stand here, resting my arm over my notepad like a child taking a test, trying to make it difficult for cheaters to get their work done.

Odessa will do the talking. She'll say, "Well, if you could excuse me, I need clean sheets for the beds." I'll move over a little bit. I'll twist to the left so she can get to the twin and queen sizes. I'm willing to move for Odessa. I can put one foot on top of the other. I'll do anything for her as long as I don't have to put my feet onto the gray carpet in the hall. I can't. I'm not ready. If I put a foot out there too early, everything will be lost.

Odessa sometimes asks me, "Which sheets do you want on your bed?" She knows I'm particular about these things. She knows her color combinations, dots and stripes together, attack me in my sleep. Sometimes I get up in the middle of the night, pull the sheets off the bed, throw them into the hall, and return to sleep. She will ask me what I want and I'll point to the plain white ones, the ones that seem lighter, cleaner than all the others. Odessa reaches for the sheets and in the instant when they're in her hand but still in the closet, I press my face into them. I press my face into the pile of sheets, into Odessa's hands underneath. I won't feel her skin, her fingers, only cool, clean fabric against my cheek. I inhale deeply as if there were a way to draw the sheets into my lungs, to hold the linen inside me. I breathe and take my head away. Odessa will pull her hands out of the closet and ask, "Do you want the door closed?" I nod. I turn away, draw in my breath, and make myself flat. She closes the door.

I'm hiding in the linen closet sending memos to myself. It's getting complicated. Odessa knows I'm here. She knows but she won't tell anybody. She won't go running into the living room and announce, "Jody's locked herself into the linen closet and she won't come out."

Odessa won't go outside and look for my father. She won't find him pulling weeds on the hill behind the house. Odessa won't tell him, "She's in there with paper, pencils, and that little light you gave her for Christmas." She won't say anything. Odessa understands that this is the way things sometimes are. She'll change the sheets on all the beds, serve the Fat Club ladies their cottage cheese and cantaloupe, and then she'll go downstairs into the bathroom and take a few sips from the bottle of Johnnie Walker she keeps there.

I'm hiding in the closet with my life suspended. I'm hiding and I'm scared to death. I want to come clean, to see myself clearly, in detail, like a hallucination, a death-bed vision, a Kodacolor photograph. I need to know if I'm alive or dead.

I'm hiding in the linen closet and I want to introduce myself to myself. I need to like what I see. If I am really as horrible as I feel, I will spontaneously combust, leaving a small heap of ashes that can be picked up with the Dustbuster. I will explode myself in a flash of fire, leaving a letter of most profuse apology.

Through the wall I hear my mother's Fat Club ladies laugh. I hear the rattle of the group and the gentle tinkling of the individual. It's as though I have more than one pair of ears. Each voice enters in a different place, with a different effect.

I hear them and realize they're laughing for me. They're celebrating the fact that I can no longer pretend. There are tears in my eyes. I'm saying thank you and good-bye. I'm writing it down because I can't simply go out there and stand at the edge of the dining room table until my mother looks up from her copy of the *Eat Yourself Slim Diet* and says, "Yes?"

I can't say that I'm leaving because she'll ask, "When will you be back?"

She'll be looking through the book, flipping through the menus, seeing how many ounces she can eat. If I tell the truth, if I say never, she'll look up at me, peering up higher than usual, above the frameless edges of her reading glasses. She'll say, "A comedian. Maybe Johnny Carson will hire you to guest-host. When will you be back?"

If I go without answering, the other ladies will watch me leave. When I get to where they think I can't hear them, when I get to the kitchen door, they'll put a pause in their meeting and talk about their children.

They'll say they were always the best parents they knew how to be. They'll say they gave their children everything and it was never enough. They'll say they hope their children will grow up and have children exactly like themselves. They'll be thinking about how their children hate them and how they hate their children back because they don't understand what it was they did wrong.

"It has nothing to do with you," I'll have to say. "It's me, it's me, all mine. There is no blame."

"Selfish," the mothers will say.

I'm here in the linen closet, doing my spring cleaning. I'm confessing right and left and Odessa knocks on the door. She knocks and then opens the door. She's carrying a plate with a sandwich and a glass of milk. Only Odessa would serve milk and a sandwich. My mother would give me a Tab with a twist of lemon. My father would make something like club soda with a little bit of syrup in it. He would use maple syrup and spend all afternoon telling me he'd invented something new, something better than other sodas because it had no chemicals, less sugar, and no caffeine. Odessa brings me a sandwich and a glass of milk and it looks like a television commercial. The bread is white, the sandwich cut perfectly in half. There are no finger marks on it, no indentations on the white bread where Odessa put her fingers while she was cutting. The glass is full except for an inch at the top. There are no spots in that inch. The milk looks white and thick, with small bubbles near the top. It looks cool and refreshing.

Odessa hands me the plate. I look at her for a moment. She is perfect. I drink the milk and know that I will have a mustache. I look at Odessa and want to say, "I love you." I want to tell her how no one else would bring me a glass of milk. I want to tell her everything, but she starts talking. Odessa says, "Make sure you don't leave that plate in the closet. I don't want your mother finding it and thinking I've lost my mind. I don't want bugs in here. Bring it out and put it in the dishwasher. Don't stay in there all day or you'll lose your color." I nod and she closes the door.

I'm hiding and I'm eating a cream-cheese-and-cucumber sandwich and having my head examined. I'm in the neighborhood of my soul and getting worried. I'm trying not to hate myself so much, trying not to hate my body, my mind, the thoughts I think. I'm hiding in the linen closet having a sex change. I'm in here with a pad of paper writing things I've thought and then unthought. Thoughts that seemed like incest, like they shouldn't be allowed.

I'm trying to find some piece of myself that is truly me, a part that I would be willing to wear like a jewel around my neck. My foot. I love my foot. If I had to send a part of myself to represent myself in some other country, or in some other way, I would amputate my foot and send it wrapped in white tissue on a silk-embroidered cushion. I would send my foot because it is me, more me than I'm willing to let on. There are other parts that are also good— hands, eyes, mouth—but after a few months I might look at them and not see the truth. After a few years I might look at them and think of someone else. But my foot is mine, all mine, the real thing. There is no mistaking it. I look at it; I take off my sock and it screams my name.

I could go on for hours demonstrating how well I know myself, through my foot, but I won't. It's embarrassing. The foot, my foot, that I wish to wear on a ribbon around my neck is an example of grace twisted and trapped. Chunks of bone and flesh conforming to the dictum: form follows function. It's a wonder I'm not a cripple.

I'm hiding in the linen closet, writing a declaration of independence. I'm in the closet, but the worst is over. There is hope, trapped inside my foot; inside my soul there is possibility. I'm looking at myself and slowly I'm falling in love. I've figured out what it takes to live forever. I'm in love and I'm free.

I want to throw the door open and hear an orchestra

swell. I want to run out to the Fat Club ladies and tell them, "Life can go on, I'm in love."

I'll stand in the living room, facing the sofa. I'll stand with my arms spread wide, the violins reaching their pitch. I'll be sweating and shaking, unsteady on my feet, my wonderful, loving, lovable feet. At the end of my proclamation my mother will let her glasses fall from her face and dangle from the cord around her neck.

"Miss Dramatic," she'll say. "Why weren't you an actress?"

The fat ladies will look at each other. They'll look at me and think of other declarations of love. They'll look and one will ask, "Who's the lucky man?"

There will be a silence while they wait for a name, preferably the right kind of a name. If I tell them it isn't a man, their silence will grow and they'll expect what they think is the worst. No one except my mother will have nerve enough to say, "A girl then?"

I'll be forced to tell them, It's not like that. One of the ladies, the one the others think isn't so smart, will ask, "What's it like?"

I'll smile, the orchestra will swell, and I'll look at the four ladies sitting on the sofa, the sofa covered with something modern and green, something that vaguely resembles the turf on a putting green.

"It's like falling in love with life itself," I'll say.

My mother will look around the room. She'll look anywhere except at me.

"Are you all right?" she'll ask when I stop to catch my breath. "You look a little flushed." I'll be singing and dancing.

"I'm fine, I'm wonderful, I'm better than before. I'm in love."

I'll sing and on the end note cymbals will crash and the sound will hold in the air for a minute. And then swinging a top hat and cane, I'll dance away. I'll dance down the hall towards the den.

I want to find my father in the den, the family room, watching tennis on television. I want to catch him in the middle of a set and say that I can't wait for a break. I want to tell him, "Life must go on."

He'll say that it's match point. He'll say that he's been trying to tell me that all along.

"But why didn't you tell me what it really means?"

"It seemed pretty obvious."

And then I'll tell him, "I'm in love." There will be a pause. Someone will have the advantage. My feet will go *clickety-clack* over the parquet floor and he'll say, "Yes, you sound very happy. You sound like you're not quite yourself."

"I'm more myself than I've ever been."

I want to find Odessa. "Life will go on," I'll tell her. "I'm in love." I'll take her by the hand and we'll dance in circles around the recreation room. We'll dance until we're dizzy and Odessa will ask me, "Are you all right?"

I'll only be able to mumble "Ummmm hummm," because my grin will have set like cement. I'm hiding in the linen closet writing love letters to myself.

ESTHER IN THE NIGHT

If something horrible happens it won't be my fault. It's the middle of the night and I'm checking things, walking around the house making sure everything is all right. I'm losing sleep. I check the thermostat, the doors, the smoke detector.

I think about a burglar. He would come up onto the porch, turn the knob, and come into my house. He would take things: the television, the VCR, the silver, my jewelry, things I've collected over the years, collected as symbols of my marriage, things that sometimes seem as though they are the marriage. I would help him pack. He would take the things that make me who I am, and then I would be able to be someone else.

A burglar would come in and kill us all. He would think of himself as a violent criminal and I would think he was doing me a favor. We would line up and for the first time in twenty years I would ask to come first: Shoot me, shoot me please. I don't have the guts to do it myself.

A burglar would wake Harold and me. He'd tell us, "Round everybody up. I want the whole house in one room." We'd go down the hall and get Cindy. The burglar would be behind us, his gun pressed into my back. We'd get to her door and find it locked from the inside. While

Harold pounded on the door, I would explain that Cindy was fifteen and that's the way things sometimes are. Harold would bang on the door. He'd scream that if she didn't open it he'd take the door off its hinges. Harold would say it was his house and he had the right to get into any room. We'd get Cindy out of her room and the burglar would say, "What about in there? What about that room there with the light on?"

I'd tell him there was no one there. He'd poke me with the gun, and ask what about the light, the Motley Crue poster on the door, and why was the radio on. "Don't play games with me, lady," he'd say.

We'd take him in. We'd go in front of him. Harold and I would lead him and then step aside. He'd see the body on the bed, the plastic tubing, the thin blue water mattress that keeps Paul constantly moving. He'd see Paul, eyes open, looking nowhere, the body twisted, or more untwisted like a pretzel undone. He'd see it all and drop everything. He'd run from our house not wanting to take anything, not wanting to hold anything that had been touched by the magic of the living dead.

A fire. Something in the basement, in the wiring, in one of the walls. Before we noticed half the house might be consumed. A wall of fire would rupture through the linen closet, eating the children's baby blankets. It would lick us in our sleep. I would feel warm dark smoke fill my lungs. In my sleep, I would cough and roll toward it breathing deeply. And Paul. Paul in a fire. His tubing would dissolve into a hot pool of plastic, it would begin to bubble, then turn black. Crystals of plastic would imbed themselves in his skin. The oxygen tank, a tall green canister that I once thought was him, would explode. From the doorway I once saw the outline of something tall and rounded, and thought of Paul bending over. I mistook a green metal tank for my son and for a moment thought everything was all right.

I check everything and go into my son's room. In the middle of the night, I watch him float somewhere between sleep and death. The shades are up. The lights are on as though we think Paul will wake up in the middle of the night and not know where he is; as if light equals life. I wonder if we leave them on so that when we check on him, we don't have to lean over the bed, the body, stretch out across our son and flick the switch. Lights are shining in Paul's face and he doesn't notice.

From the outside, from the other side of the windows, Paul's room looks like an exhibit. I've seen it at night when I'm out walking the dog. Brightly lit, he looks like something on display, a Christmas window in suburbia.

The Museum of the Modern Dead. Open twenty-four hours a day, seven days a week, admission five dollars, three for students, free to seniors, children under five, and the severely handicapped. Come one, come all, come to the birthplace of the living dead, come spend a day with us, it'll last a lifetime.

We're a working museum. I wear a period costume, like the ladies at Williamsburg. I always wear the blue, red, and purple dress I had on the night the state trooper called and said there had been an accident—my car, my son. I show visitors the telephone that rang as Harold and I were walking in the door, coming home from a dinner party. I tell them about the party, our friends, and how we used to laugh. I have index cards with the recipes Rita used that night. I hand them out while I describe listening to the trooper tell me Paul might not live until morning. I explain wearing the dress for four days and nights while we waited in the little rooms next to the intensive care and surgical suites. The dress seemed all wrong, like a piñata in a library.

I pull the visitors close and whisper in their ears that I prayed that night. I prayed for four days even though I didn't know if I believed in God. I tell them that if they're ever in a praying situation to be specific, to include certain clauses. It's not enough to assume that if a person lives he'll be all right.

I take visitors into the living room and we pause there. I unhook the red velvet ropes and have them sit on the sofa while I talk about how Harold and I wanted nothing more than for our son to get well. I talk about Paul and show baby pictures. I have pictures of his arm, broken ten years ago when he fell off his bike. I tell them I thought I'd go crazy if everything didn't come out all right, if he couldn't play football, baseball, if he couldn't do everything he wanted to do. I tell them what they already know, but still want to hear.

All we ever wanted was a normal child, happy and healthy. We told ourselves we would give anything for our children. We said this as though it was something to be proud of. I whisper everything just in case they don't want to hear it.

I pass around his medical charts, photographs of his brain, X-rays of his spinal column, graphs and charts they showed us at the hospital, words I've learned to pronounce. We talk about what it means to be in a coma, a deep sleep that lets my baby breathe, keeps his eyes open, and sometimes makes him sit bolt upright, like he's seen a ghost. I ask for questions, ask if anyone there has ever been in a coma. I ask the visitors to raise their hands.

Help. What kind of help are we getting? The doctors didn't think it was a good idea to take him home. They thought it was better for him to be in our lives from a distance, from a hospital room.

Harold put his foot down. He said, "Not one more red cent," and they said we could check him out, they'd done all they could. He was ours, we could have him back if we promised to hire help, to see a therapist, to try to rehabilitate him. We could take him home if we promised to pay our bill. I show them Harold's bill folder, his whole file cabinet crammed with computer printouts, pieces of paper with more zeros than our calculator.

Help. I talk to them about therapy, about all of us in one room, coming together to hate Paul. The shrink said we couldn't let him run our lives. She said, "Okay, let's not talk about Paul this week, let's talk about something else," but even that was about Paul, because we purposely left him out.

Cindy said, "I wish he was dead."

And everyone nodded.

I tell them about Cindy, how she showed her brother to her friends just like he showed *her* off when she was a baby. She brought her friends into his room because they asked to come. They stood around the bed in a tight cluster, and asked her where each tube went in and where it came out. They asked and finally Cindy had enough of it. She pulled down the sheets and let them look for themselves. She showed them her brother, lying naked, his legs and arms arranged in a pattern that was supposed to be good for circulation. She showed them the special motorized pad, medical Magic Fingers, that kept him moving so he wouldn't get bedsores. She showed them everything. And then she watched them staring at her brother's pale frozen body, at the way the tube came out of his penis. They would look at that part of him as long as she would let them. Cindy told me that one time a girl asked if she could touch it and Cindy said yes. She said yes and then turned away. She turned her head and out of the corner of her eye she saw the girl pull her hand back.

"It's warm," the girl said.

"He's not dead, you know," Cindy said, and the girl blushed, turned red like a maraschino cherry.

"You're gross," Cindy said, and she pulled up the sheets and tucked him in.

She tucked Paul in like he was a baby. She was gentle because she hated him.

I tell them about how my daughter came into the kitchen while I was talking on the phone. "I hate him," she said. "I hate him so much that sometimes I think I'm going to do something terrible." I told the person I was talking to I'd have to call back. "It must be so difficult for you," she said.

Cindy cried, and I told her it was all right. I told her it was perfectly normal to feel that way. I told her I felt that way too.

She said, "No, Mom, it's different, it's different for me, I've always hated him."

Welcome to the Museum. For your admission fee I show you everything, tell it all, saving the best for last. I bring you down the hall to his room. I explain that what you smell—a sweet, heavy odor, with lingering bitterness, a sharp cleanser-like aftertaste—is the perfume of the living dead. Breathe with your mouth open.

It's after four o'clock in the morning and I'm in Paul's room. I sit next to his bed and notice that if I look at just one part of him, an ankle or a hand, he doesn't seem so terribly damaged. If I look at anything bigger than a couple of inches, I see him pale and rigid, slightly puffy, frozen in a nightmare. I sit and talk to Paul and I ask him what I'm supposed to do.

"Paul?"

He doesn't answer, or tell me to get out. Paul doesn't explain things like he used to. He doesn't say he's hearing Led Zeppelin in his head and it sounds so loud that he thought for a minute the stereo was on. He doesn't tell me his head is like some sort of wonderful stereo, because there's always music in it, always the songs he wants to hear. He doesn't say he's commercial-free. I brush his hair back with my fingernails and think about how it's getting sort of long again. He doesn't pull away, doesn't say, "God, Mom, leave me alone, okay?" Paul doesn't tell me what the hell happened. He doesn't apologize.

I sit in Paul's room until I'm sure I'll do the right thing. I'm with my baby and every thought is connected to him. I know that if I just sit there, I'll stay forever.

I get up and empty his trash can. I take the bag into the kitchen and leave it by the door. I open a new box of Hefty's and go back into his room. In front of him, I open the bag, I shake it until it's filled with air. I go to Paul, pull the oxygen tube out of his nose, lift his head, and slide the bag over it. I put the bag on slowly hoping he'll stop me, twist away. I slide the bag over his head and pull it tight around his neck, wishing he'd fight. As I do it, I see myself in the mirror of his window.

I watch my reflection and when I see what I'm doing, I quickly lean over Paul and turn off the light. I stop anyone else from seeing me. The room goes black except for small red lights on Paul's machines, lights that say everything is working perfectly.

I look at Paul. I see how easy it's been to tie the bag around his head. I watch him with the bag over his head, tied around his neck. He breathes, pulling the bag up close against his features, his nose, eyes, mouth pressing against it. I watch him exhale. His breath pushes against the dark green plastic; the bag puffs out like a balloon. I close the bag tighter around him, thinking the less time it takes the better, thinking I want it over fast. I want the end.

I hold the bag while Paul breathes, and after a minute or a few minutes, he doesn't breathe as well. He breathes less, as though he's tired. He is barely breathing and I know I could still stop it. I could stop myself from becoming a murderer, but don't.

If I don't do this now, I'll regret it, and only have to do it later. Later everything will become harder and will always become harder until it's over. I push the bag into his face, into his mouth, into his nose, and finally he takes a breath, lets out a breath, and is still.

I take the bag, moist with his breath, away from him. I lift his head, pull the bag off, and close it. I sit beside his bed until I am sure the breath was his last, until I am sure he won't start breathing again when I'm not looking.

I press my head to his chest, to his lungs, his heart. I press my face to his face, there's sweat on it. I feel the skin go cold. I press my face to his face and feel him die. I sit in his room until I'm sure the end has come and gone, until morning comes. The sun comes up, crossing behind the houses at the end of the street. I sit thinking how easy it was, how simple it seemed. From now on I will always know where Paul is. I will always know how he is. I think about Cindy, Harold, my parents, and how at any moment something could happen, an incomplete accident, and again, I'd be waiting. I think about the number of Hefty bags in a box. It's six o'clock in the morning. I'm back in my bed, my body pressed against Harold's. In his sleep he wraps himself around me. I am trapped. He snores, his chest presses against my back. His breath blows on the crown of my head, a strange hot and sour breeze.

SLUMBER PARTY

In the woods behind someone's house Ben and Sally gathered leaves and lit them on fire.

Ben struck two matches at once without ripping them out of the pack. He touched the burning matches to as many leaves as he could before the whole pack ignited and burned into his fingers.

The fire grew and Ben pushed Sally back a couple of feet. "Move," he said.

The two of them stood in the leaves, sometimes in the fire, the flames sometimes reaching out to the bottoms of their jeans. Sally bent into the fire and pulled out a burning leaf. She held the leaf between two fingers and watched it dissolve into an edge of red ember that left only the hard stem in her hand.

"Get some more," Ben said. They gathered leaves again and again, moving farther into the woods each time, bending to the ground and scooping them up in their arms, carrying back what seemed like entire forests pressed to their chests.

As she bent to pick up leaves, Ben poked Sally between the legs with the stick he had used to stir the fire. She pretended to ignore him. Ben pushed the stick back and forth, rubbing it not so much against Sally's crotch as along the inside of her thighs, scratching against her jeans.

As he poked her he laughed, not a regular funny laugh, but higher-pitched, like a maniac on the loose.

Sally looked at him the same way her mother sometimes looked at her father and said, "Quit it."

They lit fires, each one bigger than the last until the flames started jumping wildly and as they stamped them out the bells of their jeans caught fire and the denim glowed red and they could feel the heat on their clean white calfs.

The woods filled with smoke and the edge of one of the fires got loose and Ben had to chase after it. Far off they heard sirens and Sally thought for sure they were for them.

Finally, when they'd scared themselves sufficiently, when both of Ben legs were covered with bright red burns so hot they felt cold, he and Sally sat down on the dirt and Sally pulled a pack of Marlboros from the hiding place in her sock.

She shook out one for each of them, then stuffed the pack back into her sock. Ben lit both cigarettes and for a minute held both between his lips smoking two at once, as though doubling the amount doubled the pleasure, doubled the fun.

"That was good," Ben said as he smoked.

Sally nodded and didn't say anything. She was practicing inhaling and didn't want to break her concentration.

"You know," Ben said, when they were finished smoking and were putting perfume that Sally had stolen from her mother between their fingers so they didn't smell like tobacco, "I like you better than Julie. Julie wears dresses."

Sally pulled a pack of gum out of her pocket and they both popped huge wads into their mouths to clean their breath.

"I hate girls who wear dresses," Ben said, as he chomped down on the gum, lips smacking.

They climbed up the hill and out of the woods. Secretly Sally smiled. Julie and Ben were a year older than she; they would be eleven before she was even ten and they were best friends.

"Sal Lee." She could hear her mother's voice over the top of the hill. It came through in broken phrases like a radio with static. "Sal Lee. Sal Lee. Come. In this house. Now."

It was late afternoon; the edge of the sun was just dropping back behind the house at the top of the hill. The TV antenna, the highest point on the block, was set off against the sky like the peak of a church and glowed like gold.

Cars with fathers coming home from work pulled into driveways, throwing shadows across chalk-drawn hop-scotch games and ending basketball tournaments by parking in the court. The echoes of metal car doors slamming shut bounced off the brick houses.

Ben and Sally walked slowly, as though they were tired.

"Sally," her mother called, her voice clear now. They were one backyard from home. "Is Ben with you?"

Sally and Ben gave each other guilty looks and wondered if they were in trouble for the fires, the smoking, or the perfume Sally stole. Neither said anything.

They came around the edge of the house, with innocent expressions spread across their faces as though they'd been Scotch-taped there.

"I've been calling you for twenty minutes," Sally's mother said. "You're sleeping over tonight, remember?" she said to Ben. "Your mother dropped off your things. She'll call later, to say good night."

Ben's father disappeared a long time ago. His parents weren't divorced, but his father just went off one day and never came back. Sometimes the police would think they found him or found a clue that would help them find him, but nothing ever came of it. Sometimes Ben's mother had meetings for work at night and if the housekeeper was off Ben spent the night at one of the houses up or down the block, wherever there was someone willing to have him.

"Because we have company tonight," Sally's mother said, making a big deal over Ben even though he ate over often enough to be called a regular, "we're using the grill."

They looked out onto the back patio where Sally's much older brother Robert was leaning over the grill, attending to the chicken pieces with the kind of precision and commitment seen only in boys in their very late teens who are determined once and for all to do something right.

He didn't look up when his mother called him.

"Robert," she said over and over again and she tapped on the glass door to the patio. "Robert, how much longer?"

"Seven minutes, maybe seven and a half," he said.

Ben looked out at Robert. Robert was taller than anyone he knew, and thinner than anyone he'd ever seen. Ben stood at the kitchen door watching him, until finally Robert took the chicken off the grill and brought it inside.

"Dinner's ready," Sally's mother said. Sally's father came out from the den, and Ben and Sally washed their hands and dried them on a dish towel while Robert looked on with mild disgust.

"Your nails," he said to no one in particular. But Ben went back to the sink and washed his hands again, this time scraping his nails back and forth against the soap, leaving five troughs in the Ivory.

The conversation at dinner somehow took Ben away from Sally and divided them into sides, male against female. Sally didn't like it. She didn't like being lumped together with her mother and treated like a maid. She just wanted to sit there like everyone else. She hated her father for telling her to get up and get the salt, and Robert for saying, "While you're at it, get some ice cubes," and her father even more for saying, to Ben, "Is there anything you need while Sally is up?"

After dinner, Robert and his father balled up their napkins, threw them into the middle of their plates, and got up from the table. Ben sat at the empty table and waited for Sally to finish helping her mother with the dishes.

When everything was washed and dried they were allowed out again. The sky had dropped down into the shade of blue where everything is still, the moment just before night.

"Don't go out of the yard," Sally's mother said.

Ben and Sally hid behind the metal storage shed in the carport and shared a cigarette.

Ben tried a new thing where he took a deep drag and exhaled straight into Sally's mouth as she inhaled and then when she exhaled there was nothing left.

"Let me do it to you," Sally whispered.

Ben shook his head and took a drag and this time kept it for himself.

Through the screen door, they heard her mother asking Robert, "Are you sure you turned the grill off? I feel like I smell something burning."

They each took one last drag and then Ben put the cigarette out on the bottom of his shoe and Sally jammed the half-smoked Marlboro back into the pack and hid them again in her sock.

Sally's mother came to the door, opened it, and called Sally's name. Behind the storage shed Ben and Sally held their breath and waited.

"Sally," her mother called again.

Ben's foot slipped and he fell against the metal shed, with a thud that sounded like the shed had burped.

"Five more minutes," Sally's mother said, going back into the house and letting the screen door close behind her.

Sally pushed Ben into the shed and again it made the same burping noise.

"Great," Sally said, and she popped gum in her mouth and rubbed White Linen between her fingers.

"Gimmie gum," Ben said.

Sally threw him a piece, which landed in a puddle on the ground.

"Another one," Ben said.

"Sorry, last piece." And Ben picked the gum out of the puddle, wiped it on his shirt sleeve, and put it in his mouth.

"I've made up beds for the two of you in the extra room downstairs," Sally's mother said.

Actually "downstairs" was the basement.

"I don't want to be kept up all night with your horsing around," she said.

Sally looked at Ben. The basement scared her. She didn't even like going down there during the day and certainly never planned to sleep there.

"We can stay in my room," Sally said. "We'll be quiet."

Sally's mother shook her head.

"Then Ben can sleep in Robert's room," Sally said.

Ben stood in the hall between Sally and her mother, feeling uncomfortable, and unwanted.

"Robert's too old to be having people sleeping in his room," Sally's mother said, patting Ben on the head. "You'll be fine downstairs. Wash up and get into your pajamas, then you can watch TV for half an hour."

All during their TV show Sally thought about sleeping in the basement. She thought about the big closets in the recreation room. She thought about the furnace room and what might be in there. She thought about being downstairs in the darkness so far from everyone asleep upstairs. If she was scared she couldn't tell Ben because he'd think she was being a baby, or worse, a girl. All during the TV show, she thought about staying awake all night.

"Good night," her mother said to her as she kissed her forehead.

All three stood at the top of the stairs.

"I put extra blankets down there in case it gets chilly. Don't stay up all night," Sally's mother said.

Sally was holding Robert's old flashlight and kept flicking it off and on with her thumb.

Her mother looked down at Sally. "I put a night-light on down there." Sally shrugged. "Good night," her mother said, kissing her again and then kissing Ben even though he pretended to pull away.

"What are those red marks on your leg?" she asked Ben.

Ben looked down at his burns. "Poison ivy," he said.

"Well, just don't scratch," Sally's mother said.

"Ben and Sally went quietly downstairs, Sally following Ben. The recreation room was dark except for the glow of the night-light, which threw long shadows across the cool linoleum floor. There was enough light for Sally to see her reflection in the sliding glass door. She pressed her face up to the glass and tried to look out but saw nothing except her face pressed close against the glass, Ben standing behind her, and blackness beyond that.

The trundle bed, pushed against the wall under a window, was all made up. It looked small, lost in the big room.

"Pick," Ben said, and Sally couldn't decide which was

better, safer, the higher or the lower; near the floor where a burglar or killer might not notice her but where something could crawl across her in her sleep, or up in the air at normal height, but unprotected, vulnerable to the night and the big room.

"I'll sleep down here," Sally said, picking the lower bed.

She pulled back the covers, looked for crawly things, and then got in, pulling the blanket to her chin and from the inside pulling it tight around her like she was burying herself.

"What's in there," Ben said, pointing to the furnace room door.

"Why?" Sally said.

"I thought I heard something."

"It's just the furnace," Sally said.

"It sounded like a man," Ben said.

And Sally hated Ben.

"A man with a hook instead of an arm, scratching to get out."

Ben was silent. Sally kept thinking that she could just run upstairs. She could just jump out of the bed and run screaming upstairs and if she screamed enough they wouldn't make her come back down. Ben would hate her but she wouldn't care.

"Did you hear it?" Ben asked.

He was silent and then he started laughing.

He started laughing and laughing and he fell off the bed laughing and finally he was snorting and laughing and when he couldn't breathe anymore he stopped laughing and just sat up on the high bed smiling at himself.

" 'Night," Sally said, and she pulled the sheet up over her ears and turned so she could keep an eye on the furnace room door, but it was hard because there was a window behind her and she felt like she should be looking that way too.

—

With no warning Ben pulled up his nightshirt, held it up under his chin, pulled down the front of his underpants, and turned the flashlight on himself.

"Look at my boner," he said to Sally.

The last penis Sally had seen belonged to someone she'd played doctor with in the downstairs bathroom of his parents' house when his testicles were the size of green grapes and his penis was like a crayon stub at the point where you don't bother sharpening it again, you just throw it out.

"When I'm older," Ben said, "I'll have hair." Ben swayed back and forth, thrusting his penis into the air.

Sally sat up on the trundle bed and stared.

She fixed on the way this part of Ben seemed separate from the rest of his body. It stuck up and out like the gearshift in Robert's Carmen Ghia.

Ben pointed his thing towards her and Sally made a sharp sound. Ben laughed and it bounced slightly.

"When it's like this I can't pee," he said.

Sally was impressed with Ben's knowledge and the way he presented it, as though he were the exhibit in a science class.

"Touch it," he said.

She shook her head.

Ben's underwear hung down around his ankles and he stepped out of it.

"I have a hair," Sally said.

"No you don't," Ben said.

Sally shrugged.

"Let me see," he said.

"No."

As far as Sally was concerned there was nothing to pull up her nightgown for. She had nothing to show except for the lone hair. She had nothing and was increasingly aware of both the nothingness and Ben's interest in the empty space.

Ben just stood there. He thought Sally was being stupid and Sally knew it.

"Okay," she said. "But don't touch me."

Sally lay down, lifted her nightgown, and pulled her underwear down to her knees.

Ben moved in closer. "Where's the hair?" he said, shining the light on her.

Sally raised her head and looked down at herself, tripling her chin. It was there before but now she couldn't find it.

"You don't have one."

"I do so."

"Maybe it's inside," he said.

Ben pulled her underwear the rest of the way down. Sally was surprised but didn't say anything.

"Move your legs apart," Ben said.

Sally turned her head away from Ben and spread her legs. She looked at the furnace room door and imagined that the man with one arm was in there looking at her through the slats. She tried to stare at him.

Sally spread her legs and Ben stood at the end of the bed—his shirt down but caught on his erection—looking carefully at the inside of Sally.

"I don't see one," he said.

"Well, it was there before," Sally said.

Ben shrugged and moved in a little closer. "It looks like a peach pit in there."

Sally tried to remember what a peach pit looked like. She looked at Ben's face to see if he was making fun of her. His expression was serious and intent. He had the flashlight in one hand and was bent over her, almost into her, with his other hand pressed into the mattress between her legs, keeping him propped up. He examined her carefully, as though he was looking for something in particular that he just hadn't found yet.

She started to pull her nightgown down but Ben caught her arms and stopped her.

"I'm not done yet," Ben said. And he held Sally's arms until she relaxed and lay back on the bed with her nightgown gathered around her belly button and her underwear on the linoleum floor.

"Let's see your boobs," Ben said.

"I don't have any yet," Sally said in an annoyed tone. She was not happy with Ben.

"Let me see." Ben started to yank her nightgown up but Sally stopped him and did it herself.

Her breasts stuck out from her body just enough to look like a fat boy's chest; there was nothing female or sexy about them. The nipples were puffy soft spots that looked slanted like Chinese eyes and sometimes felt like bruises.

She lay naked with Ben standing over her, and in their nakedness whatever they knew about how to move, how to walk or talk, completely disappeared.

The recreation room was spread out underneath the whole house. They could hear footsteps, muffled TV voices, water running, and Sally's father locking the front door.

"Let's do it," Ben said, softly.

Sally knew what he was getting at but thought it was one of those things like reading the newspaper that you just didn't do until you were grown up. She wasn't as big on taking chances as she liked to think she was. Sally shook her head.

Ben pulled his nightshirt off. Sally looked at his nipples, small and flat like dimes.

"Oh, come on," Ben said. "You're no fun."

And they were stuck there, silent, waiting, staring at

each other's nakedness until finally Sally said, "All right."

"All right," she said, and rolled over onto her stomach and poked her butt up into the air.

"What are you doing?" Ben asked.

"Go ahead," she said.

"That's not how you do it," Ben said.

"Yes it is," Sally said and she stayed like that for about five minutes with Ben just watching her and both of them feeling more confused than they were willing to admit.

Suddenly they both saw something outside. It was a strange kind of something; a flicker of light, not white light like the flashlight, but red-orange light like a fire.

"Let's go outside," Ben said just as Sally was thinking they should go upstairs and beg to be allowed to sleep up there.

Sally shook her head.

"Come on," Ben said. "We have to." And even though Sally couldn't imagine why they should go outside in the middle of the night, especially when they had just seen something out there, she was glad to be able to move.

There was something strange about the way Ben said "we have to," as though whatever they had seen out there had something to do with them and they had to go outside and face it.

She started to put on her nightgown but Ben grabbed it and pulled it off her.

"No," he said. "Naked."

"I don't want to," Sally said.

Ben took her arms and pulled her to the sliding glass door that led outside. It was dark out. Sally didn't like the dark.

"Are you scared?" Ben asked. Sally shook her head.

"I just don't want to."

"We have to," Ben said.

Sally believed him. He took her hand and they walked towards the door.

Ben and Sally stood naked in the night, in the grass just beyond the back patio of Sally's house. They stood five feet apart, facing out into the woods. The woods behind Sally's house were part of the same stretch of woods that spread out behind all the houses on the street. They were a piece of the same woods that Ben and Sally had set on fire.

They stood, without realizing it, directly under Sally's parents' bedroom windows, which were open to the night air. They were silent, hypnotized by the sensation of the air on their naked bodies.

Ben's erection stuck out in front of him like a compass or a divining stick. In the breeze it seemed alternately to shrink slightly and then get bigger than before, beating like a pulse. Ben touched himself. He couldn't resist. He put his fingers around the head and rubbed a little bit. Sally saw him, watched him, and it was as though by touching himself—or maybe by not asking her to do it for him—he'd somehow broken the bond between them and had betrayed her. She didn't say anything, but when Ben noticed her watching he stopped and let his hands fall to his sides.

The woods beyond the patio were pitch dark, and so were the backyards to the left and right. Through the darkness and the leaves on the trees they could see lights on in houses far away. The breeze blew the leaves and the lights seemed to flicker like fires.

There was a small noise, heavier than a breeze but still very light, nothing to be afraid of. Ben and Sally looked at each other but were not scared—or were already too scared to be any more scared. The noise got louder, leaves moving, maybe an animal walking, and then they heard voices.

Ben and Sally stood tranquilized by their bath in the night. Neither had the power or desire to move. Two tall figures stepped out from the darkness, stepped out from behind the brick wall that separated the patio from the rest of the backyard. Sally immediately recognized the two figures as someone's older brothers, but couldn't remember whose. Ben knew them and kind of let one of his knees relax as if trying to assume a casual pose. In a way he was proud to be out there naked with Sally. His hard-on stood apart from him, independent, as though it had a life and a mind of its own; he tried to ignore it.

The two young men were carrying things, a television set, a large radio, a big bag, and other things that weren't clear in the darkness. They stood directly in front of Ben and Sally, facing them each one on one. With the two boys there, somehow Ben and Sally were no longer together but stood alone. The four of them stood wordless in the backyard.

One of the boys put down the TV he was carrying, pulled a cigarette from his shirt pocket, and lit it. They all breathed deeply, inhaling the smell. The cigarette glowed, flaring as the boy inhaled. He took a couple of drags and then handed the cigarette to Ben—whose erection, Sally noticed, seemed to be sinking. Ben smoked the cigarette.

"Honey, do you smell something burning?" Sally's mother said.

Through the house and the night her voice sounded distant and far away.

Ben dropped the cigarette on the ground in front of him. The boy in front of him reached his sneakered foot out and crushed the cigarette into the grass. The four of them stood, completely motionless and breathless, waiting to be caught.

But there were no sounds other than the wind in the trees and no lights came on anywhere and after a minute they all started breathing again and thought they were safe.

The boy facing Sally put down the TV and the bag he was carrying. He reached out to Sally, his fingers sort of pinching together in the air. He reached for her breast, or the start of what would later be her breast, but changed his mind. The backs of his fingers brushed against her nipple for a second and Sally felt strange.

He lowered his hand, extended his index finger, and gently pushed into the break between Sally's legs. He left his finger there, not inside, not outside, but held in the flesh of the slit.

Sally looked at Ben and saw that he had his erection back. Sally felt the finger there, felt the rest of the fingers and the hand outside her. It was as though someone had asked her to do a magic trick, to hold a pencil in her crotch for a minute or more.

In time the boy pulled his finger out and as he did Sally could feel his fingernail lightly scraping her insides.

After the boy pulled his finger out, he picked up the TV and the bag, looked at the other boy, and they both walked into the darkness.

Ben and Sally turned and went inside. Sally could still feel the imprint of the finger when she sat back down on the trundle bed. She felt the feeling of the finger and rocked back and forth on the sensation of the finger having been there.

"You can't say anything" was all Ben said to her. "There's no way to explain, so you can't say anything."

They sat naked for a minute in their beds and then it seemed too dark, too cold, and too late to be that way and so they put their clothing on again.

"Where's my underpants?" Sally said.

Ben shrugged. He was tired and overwhelmed.

"I need them," Sally said.

She made Ben move the beds so they could look under them and behind them and she started to get a little hysterical and Ben got mad and told her to "calm the fuck down." Sally got in bed and tried to sleep, but the sensation of being naked under the nightgown with the fingerprint was too much and at a certain point, in the middle of the night, after Ben had fallen asleep, she had to go upstairs for underwear.

From the end of the dark hall she heard the steady rumble of her father snoring; his deep ragged inhalations worked like a magnet, pulling her down the hall towards her room.

Before entering her room, Sally reached in and turned the light on. Her underwear drawer opened with a loud wooden squeak which woke her mother.

"What are you doing?" her mother asked in a sleepy voice from the next room.

"Getting something," Sally said.

"Go to sleep," her mother said in as much of an angry voice as a sleeping mother could manage.

Sally stood in the center of her well-lit room and pulled on her underpants. She felt better, protected in the light, in her room, with the elastic around her waist and legs, the thicker cotton crotch pressed against her, covering her and the fingerprint like a blanket.

Sally stood, a child in her room, safe with her parents in the room next door. All she wanted to do was stay there, crawl into her bed, pull her Huggy Bear close, and sleep until her mother came in the next morning and kissed her forehead again and again until she was awake.

"Go back downstairs," her mother said.

Sally left the underwear drawer half open and went out of her room, only remembering to turn out her light when her mother mumbled, "Turn out the light."

The hall seemed darker than ever and Sally couldn't see anything. She pressed her hands against the wall and just stood there for a minute. Ben was asleep downstairs and as much as she wanted him to be awake she didn't want to wake him up. She wondered if they'd remembered to lock the back door, and thought that the boy from outside or someone worse, the man in the furnace room, would be waiting for her on the steps, or down there in the basement, and would do something to her, she didn't think what.

On her way downstairs, she passed the bay window in the living room. Sally stopped and looked outside. The streetlight at the end of the driveway lit the road like part of a movie set. Outside there was something red and glowing. Sally pressed against the glass and saw red lights silently flashing in front of the house that she and Ben had hidden behind to light their fires. The flashing red lights were mounted on top of a police car and Sally thought she and Ben hadn't put out the fires well enough; they were still burning in the backyard, the woods glowing red embers like a barbecue. Sally thought the people in the house had seen them either setting fires or maybe out there naked in the night and were turning them in.

She stood fixed in the bay window, looking out. Another police car drove slowly down the block, scanning the houses with a white searchlight mounted on the hood. The searchlight, like a flashlight, carefully examined the fronts of all the houses and then turned itself on the other

police car. Sally saw policemen and two tall figures leaning against the car and a TV and a bag on the ground,
along with other stuff that wasn't clear against the night.

The searchlight rotated around again and she felt it
sweep over her. Sally felt the light over her nightgown.
She could feel the finger in her crotch and the light finding it there. Sally felt the light catching her in the dark
living room. The light swept over again and Sally dodged
it, running downstairs ahead of it. Her feet landed hard on
every step, causing the people in the house to roll over in
their sleep and try to get comfortable again.

THE I OF IT

I am sitting naked on a kitchen chair, staring at it. My jeans and underwear are bunched up at my ankles. I walked from the bathroom to here, shuffling one foot in front of the other as though in shackles.

This has been a terrible week. I have been to the doctor. It is evening and I am sitting at my table staring down. I half wish that it had done what was threatened most in cases of severe abuse and fallen off. If I had found it lying loose under the sheets or pushed down to the bottom of the bed, rubbing up against my ankle, I could have picked it up lovingly, longingly. I could have brought it to eye level and given it the kind of inspection it truly deserved; I would have admired it from every angle, and then kept it in my dresser drawer.

I have an early memory of discovering this part of myself, discovering it as something neither my mother or sisters had. I played with it, knowing mine was the only one in the house, admiring its strength, enjoying how its presence seemed to mean so much to everyone. They were always in one way or another commenting on its existence from the manner in which they avoided it when they dried me from the tub to the way they looked out the car window when we stopped on long road trips and I stood by the highway releasing a thin yellow stream that danced in the wind.

This stub of maleness was what set me apart in a house of women; it was what comforted me most in that same house, knowing that I would never be like them.

From the time I first noticed that it filled me with warmth as I twirled my fingers over its top, I felt I had a friend. I walked to and from school and noisily up and down the stairs in our house, carrying it with me, slightly ahead of me, sharing its confidence.

I was a beautiful boy, or so they said. If I stood in my school clothes in front of the mirror I did not see anything special. My haircut was awful, my ears stuck out like telephone receivers, my eyes, while blue, seemed to disappear entirely when I smiled. And yet when I stood in front of the same mirror naked, I danced at the sight of myself, incredibly and inexcusably male.

I had no desire to be beautiful or good. Somehow, I suspect because it did not come naturally, I longed to be bad. I wanted to misbehave, to prove to myself that I could stand the sudden loss of my family's affection. I wanted to do terrible, horrible things and then be excused simply because I was a boy and that's what boys do, especially boys without fathers. I had the secret desire to frighten others. But I was forever a pink-skinned child, with straight blond hair, new khaki pants, white socks, and brown shoes.

My only true fear was of men. Having grown up without fathers, brothers, or uncles, men were completely unfamiliar to me, their naked selves only accidently seen in bathhouses or public restrooms. They lived behind extra long zippers, hidden, like something in a freak show you'd pay to see once and only once. Their ungraceful parts hung deeply down, buried in a weave of hair that wound itself denser as it got closer as if to protect the world from

the sight of such a monster. As I grew older, I taught myself to enjoy what was frightening.

I never wore underwear. Inside my jeans, it lay naked,
rubbing the blue denim white. I went out in the evenings
to roam among men, to display myself, to parade, to hunt.
I was what everyone wanted, white, clean, forever a boy.
They wanted to ruin me as a kind of revenge. It was part
of my image to look unavailable but the truth was anyone
could have me. I liked ugly men. Grab your partner and
do-si-do. Change partners. I kissed a million of them. I
opened myself to them and them to me. I walked down
the street nearly naked with it in the lead. It was pure love
in the sense of loving oneself and loving the sensation.

I was alive, incredibly, joyously. Even in the grocery
store or the laundromat, every time someone's eyes
passed over me, holding me for a second, I felt a boost that
sent me forward and made me capable of doing anything.
Every hour held a sensuous moment, a romantic possibility. Each person who looked at me and smiled, cared for
me. To be treasured by those who weren't related, to
whom I meant nothing, was the highest form of a compliment.

Men, whose faces I didn't recognize, bent down to kiss
me as I sat eating lunch in sidewalk cafes. I kissed them
back and whispered, It was good seeing you. And when
my lunch dates asked who that was, I simply smiled.

I felt celebrated. Every dream was a possibility. It was
as though I would never be afraid again. I remember
being happy.

I look down on it and begin to weep. I do not understand what has happened or why. I am sickened by
myself, and yet cannot stand the sensation of being
so revolted. It is me, I tell myself. It is me, as though familiarity should be a comfort.

I remember when the men I met were truly strangers;

our private parts went off in search of each other like dogs on a leash sniffing each other while the owners look away. I remember still, after that, meeting a man, and looking at him, looking at him days and months in a row and each time loving him.

I feel like I should wear rubber gloves for fear of touching myself or someone else. I have never felt so dangerous. I am weeping and it frightens me.

A friend told me about a group of men who make each other feel better, more hopeful, good about their bodies.

I picture a room full of men, sitting on folding chairs. They begin as any sort of meeting that welcomes strangers; they go around the room, first names only. They talk a little bit, and then finally, as though the talking is the obligatory introductory prayer, the warning of what is to follow, the cue to begin the incantation, they slowly take off their clothing, sweaters and shoes first. They silently stand up, and drop their pants to the floor. The sight of a circle of naked men and folding chairs is exciting. Those who can, rise to the occasion and fire their poison jets into the air. It is wonderful. A great relief. They are saying something. They are angry. Men shuffle around in a circle doing it until they collapse. I imagine that one time someone died at a meeting. He came and he died. When he fell, the group used it as inspiration. They did it again, over him, and it was all so much better then.

I can no longer love. I cannot possess myself as I did before. I can never again possess it, as it possessed me.

I am in my apartment screaming at nothing. This is the most horrible thing that ever happened. I am furious. I deserve better than this. I am a good boy. Truly I am. I am sorry. I am so sorry.

I look down on it and it seems to look up at me. I want it

to apologize for wanting the world, literally. I have the strongest desire to punish it, to whack it until it screams, beat it until it is bloody and runs off to hide, shaking in a corner, but I can't. I cannot turn my back so quickly, and besides it is already lying there pale and weak, as if it is dead.

I see sick men, friends that have shriveled into strangers, unwelcome in hospitals and at home. They can't think or breathe, and still as they go rattling towards death, it never loses an ounce, it lies fattened, untouched in the darkness between their legs. It is strikingly an ornament, a reminder of the past.

Should I ask for a divorce? A separation from myself on the grounds that this part of me that is more male than I alone could ever be has betrayed me. We no longer have anything in common except profound depression and disbelief. I have lost my best friend, my playmate from childhood, myself. I have lost what I loved most deeply. I wish to be compensated.

I let a napkin from the table fall across it, and then quickly whisk it away, *Voilà*, like I am doing a magic trick. I look down upon my lap as if expecting to see a bunch of flowers or a white rabbit in its place.

I remember the first man who unzipped my pants while I stood motionless, eyes turned down. I allowed myself to peek, to see it in his hand.

"It is a beautiful thing," he said, lifting it like a treasure and touching it gently.

I kick off my jeans and run from room to room. I look out onto the city that once seemed so big and has now shrunken so that it is no more than a garden surrounding my apartment. I stand naked in the window, my hands flat against the glass. My reflection is clear. There is no escaping myself. My lips press against the window. I am a beautiful boy. I feel the familiar warmth that rises when I am being taken in. In the apartment directly across from mine I see a man watching me, his hand upon himself. He seems wonderful through the glass, someone I could be with forever. He smiles. I slide the window open and lean towards the air. I am no longer safe. I step up onto the sill and spring forward into the night.

A REAL DOLL

I'm dating Barbie. Three afternoons a week, while my sister is at dance class, I take Barbie away from Ken. I'm practicing for the future.

At first I sat in my sister's room watching Barbie, who lived with Ken, on a doily, on top of the dresser.

I was looking at her but not really looking. I was looking, and all of the sudden realized she was staring at me.

She was sitting next to Ken, his khaki-covered thigh absently rubbing her bare leg. He was rubbing her, but she was staring at me.

"Hi," she said.

"Hello," I said.

"I'm Barbie," she said, and Ken stopped rubbing her leg.

"I know."

"You're Jenny's brother."

I nodded. My head was bobbing up and down like a puppet on a weight.

"I really like your sister. She's sweet," Barbie said. "Such a good little girl. Especially lately, she makes herself so pretty, and she's started doing her nails."

I wondered if Barbie noticed that Miss Wonderful bit her nails and that when she smiled her front teeth were covered with little flecks of purple nail polish. I wondered if she knew Jennifer colored in the chipped chewed spots with purple magic marker, and then sometimes sucked on her fingers so that not only did she have purple flecks of polish on her teeth, but her tongue was the strangest shade of violet.

"So listen," I said. "Would you like to go out for a while? Grab some fresh air, maybe take a spin around the backyard?"

"Sure," she said.

I picked her up by her feet. It sounds unusual but I was too petrified to take her by the waist. I grabbed her by the ankles and carried her off like a Popsicle stick.

As soon as we were out back, sitting on the porch of what I used to call my fort, but which my sister and parents referred to as the playhouse, I started freaking. I was suddenly and incredibly aware that I was out with Barbie. I didn't know what to say.

"So, what kind of a Barbie are you?" I asked.

"Excuse me?"

"Well, from listening to Jennifer I know there's Day to Night Barbie, Magic Moves Barbie, Gift-Giving Barbie, Tropical Barbie, My First Barbie, and more."

"I'm Tropical," she said. I'm Tropical, she said, the same way a person might say I'm Catholic or I'm Jewish. "I came with a one-piece bathing suit, a brush, and a ruffle you can wear so many ways," Barbie squeaked.

She actually squeaked. It turned out that squeaking was Barbie's birth defect. I pretended I didn't hear it.

We were quiet for a minute. A leaf larger than Barbie fell from the maple tree above us and I caught it just before it would have hit her. I half expected her to squeak, "You saved my life. I'm yours, forever." Instead she said, in a perfectly normal voice, "Wow, big leaf."

I looked at her. Barbie's eyes were sparkling blue like

the ocean on a good day. I looked and in a moment noticed she had the whole world, the cosmos, drawn in makeup above and below her eyes. An entire galaxy, clouds, stars, a sun, the sea, painted onto her face. Yellow, blue, pink, and a million silver sparkles.

We sat looking at each other, looking and talking and then not talking and looking again. It was a stop-and-start thing with both of us constantly saying the wrong thing, saying anything, and then immediately regretting having said it.

It was obvious Barbie didn't trust me. I asked her if she wanted something to drink.

"Diet Coke," she said. And I wondered why I'd asked.

I went into the house, upstairs into my parents' bathroom, opened the medicine cabinet, and got a couple of Valiums. I immediately swallowed one. I figured if I could be calm and collected, she'd realize I wasn't going to hurt her. I broke another Valium into a million small pieces, dropped some slivers into Barbie's Diet Coke, and swished it around so it'd blend. I figured if we could be calm and collected together, she'd be able to trust me even sooner. I was falling in love in a way that had nothing to do with love.

"So, what's the deal with you and Ken?" I asked later after we'd loosened up, after she'd drunk two Diet Cokes, and I'd made another trip to the medicine cabinet.

She giggled. "Oh, we're just really good friends."

"What's the deal with him really, you can tell me, I mean, is he or isn't he?"

"Ish she or ishn' she," Barbie said, in a slow slurred way, like she was so intoxicated that if they made a Breathalizer for Valium, she'd melt it.

I regretted having fixed her a third Coke. I mean if she o.d.'ed and died Jennifer would tell my mom and dad for sure.

"Is he a faggot or what?"

Barbie laughed and I almost slapped her. She looked me straight in the eye.

"He lusts after me," she said. "I come home at night and he's standing there, waiting. He doesn't wear underwear, you know. I mean, isn't that strange, Ken doesn't own any underwear. I heard Jennifer tell her friend that they don't even make any for him. Anyway, he's always there waiting, and I'm like, Ken we're friends, okay, that's it. I mean, have you ever noticed, he has molded plastic hair. His head and his hair are all one piece. I can't go out with a guy like that. Besides, I don't think he'd be up for it if you know what I mean. Ken is not what you'd call well endowed. . . . All he's got is a little plastic bump, more of a hump, really, and what the hell are you supposed to do with that?"

She was telling me things I didn't think I should hear and all the same, I was leaning into her, like if I moved closer she'd tell me more. I was taking every word and holding it for a minute, holding groups of words in my head like I didn't understand English. She went on and on, but I wasn't listening.

The sun sank behind the playhouse, Barbie shivered, excused herself, and ran around back to throw up. I asked her if she felt okay. She said she was fine, just a little tired, that maybe she was coming down with the flu or something. I gave her a piece of a piece of gum to chew and took her inside.

On the way back to Jennifer's room I did something Barbie almost didn't forgive me for. I did something which not only shattered the moment, but nearly wrecked the possibility of our having a future together.

In the hallway between the stairs and Jennifer's room, I popped Barbie's head into my mouth, like lion and tamer, God and Godzilla.

I popped her whole head into my mouth, and Barbie's hair separated into single strands like Christmas tinsel and caught in my throat nearly choking me. I could taste layer on layer of makeup, Revlon, Max Factor, and Maybelline. I closed my mouth around Barbie and could feel her breath in mine. I could hear her screams in my throat. Her teeth, white, Pearl Drops, Pepsodent, and the whole Osmond family, bit my tongue and the inside of my cheek like I might accidently bite myself. I closed my mouth around her neck and held her suspended, her feet uselessly kicking the air in front of my face.

Before pulling her out, I pressed my teeth lightly into her neck, leaving marks Barbie described as scars of her assault, but which I imagined as a New Age necklace of love.

"I have never, ever in my life been treated with such utter disregard," she said as soon as I let her out.

She was lying. I knew Jennifer sometimes did things with Barbie. I didn't mention that once I'd seen Barbie hanging from Jennifer's ceiling fan, spinning around in great wide circles, like some imitation Superman.

"I'm sorry if I scared you."

"Scared me!" she squeaked.

She went on squeaking, a cross between the squeal when you let the air out of a balloon and a smoke alarm with weak batteries. While she was squeaking, the phrase *a head in the mouth is worth two in the bush* started running through my head. I knew it had come from somewhere, started as something else, but I couldn't get it right. *A head in the mouth is worth two in the bush,* again and again, like the punch line to some dirty joke.

"Scared me. Scared me. Scared me!" Barbie squeaked louder and louder until finally she had my attention again. "Have you ever been held captive in the dark cavern of someone's body?"

I shook my head. It sounded wonderful.

"Typical," she said. "So incredibly, typically male."

For a moment I was proud.

"Why do you have to do things you know you shouldn't, and worse, you do them with a light in your eye, like you're getting some weird pleasure that only another boy would understand. You're all the same," she said. "You're all Jack Nicholson."

I refused to put her back in Jennifer's room until she forgave me, until she understood that I'd done what I did with only the truest of feeling, no harm intended.

I heard Jennifer's feet clomping up the stairs. I was running out of time.

"You know I'm really interested in you," I said to Barbie.

"Me too," she said, and for a minute I wasn't sure if she meant she was interested in herself or me.

"We should do this again," I said. She nodded.

I leaned down to kiss Barbie. I could have brought her up to my lips, but somehow it felt wrong. I leaned down to kiss her and the first thing I got was her nose in my mouth. I felt like a St. Bernard saying hello.

No matter how graceful I tried to be, I was forever licking her face. It wasn't a question of putting my tongue in her ear or down her throat, it was simply literally trying not to suffocate her. I kissed Barbie with my back to Ken and then turned around and put her on the doily right next to him. I was tempted to drop her down on Ken, to mash her into him, but I managed to restrain myself.

"That was fun," Barbie said. I heard Jennifer in the hall.

"Later," I said.

Jennifer came into the room and looked at me.

"What?" I said.

"It's my room," she said.

"There was a bee in it. I was killing it for you."

"A bee. I'm allergic to bees. Mom, Mom," she

screamed. "There's a bee."

"Mom's not home. I killed it."

"But there might be another one."

"So call me and I'll kill it."

"But if it stings me I might die." I shrugged and walked out. I could feel Barbie watching me leave.

I took a Valium about twenty minutes before I picked her up the next Friday. By the time I went into Jennifer's room, everything was getting easier.

"Hey," I said when I got up to the dresser.

She was there on the doily with Ken, they were back to back, resting against each other, legs stretched out in front of them.

Ken didn't look at me. I didn't care.

"You ready to go?" I asked. Barbie nodded. "I thought you might be thirsty." I handed her the Diet Coke I'd made for her.

I'd figured Barbie could take a little less than an eighth of a Valium without getting totally senile. Basically, I had to give her Valium crumbs since there was no way to cut one that small.

She took the Coke and drank it right in front of Ken. I kept waiting for him to give me one of those I-know-what-you're-up-to-and-I-don't-like-it looks, the kind my father gives me when he walks into my room without knocking and I automatically jump twenty feet in the air.

Ken acted like he didn't even know I was there. I hated him.

"I can't do a lot of walking this afternoon," Barbie said.

I nodded. I figured no big deal since mostly I seemed to be carrying her around anyway.

"My feet are killing me," she said.

I was thinking about Ken.

"Don't you have other shoes?"

My family was very into shoes. No matter what seemed to be wrong my father always suggested it could be cured by wearing a different pair of shoes. He believed that shoes, like tires, should be rotated.

"It's not the shoes," she said. "It's my toes."

"Did you drop something on them?" My Valium wasn't working. I was having trouble making small talk. I needed another one.

"Jennifer's been chewing on them."

"What?"

"She chews on my toes."

"You let her chew your footies?"

I couldn't make sense out of what she was saying. I was thinking about not being able to talk, needing another or maybe two more Valiums, yellow adult-strength Pez.

"Do you enjoy it?" I asked.

"She literally bites down on them, like I'm flank steak or something," Barbie said. "I wish she'd just bite them off and have it over with. This is taking forever. She's chewing and chewing, more like gnawing at me."

"I'll make her stop. I'll buy her some gum, some tobacco or something, a pencil to chew on."

"Please don't say anything. I wouldn't have told you except . . . ," Barbie said.

"But she's hurting you."

"It's between Jennifer and me."

"Where's it going to stop?" I asked.

"At the arch, I hope. There's a bone there, and once she realizes she's bitten the soft part off, she'll stop."

"How will you walk?"

"I have very long feet."

I sat on the edge of my sister's bed, my head in my hands. My sister was biting Barbie's feet off and Barbie didn't seem to care. She didn't hold it against her and in a way I liked her for that. I liked the fact she understood how we all have little secret habits that seem normal enough to us, but which we know better than to mention out loud. I started imagining things I might be able to get away with.

"Get me out of here," Barbie said. I slipped Barbie's shoes off. Sure enough, someone had been gnawing at her. On her left foot the toes were dangling and on the right, half had been completely taken off. There were tooth marks up to her ankles. "Let's not dwell on this," Barbie said.

I picked Barbie up. Ken fell over backwards and Barbie made me straighten him up before we left. "Just because you know he only has a bump doesn't give you permission to treat him badly," Barbie whispered.

I fixed Ken and carried Barbie down the hall to my room. I held Barbie above me, tilted my head back, and lowered her feet into my mouth. I felt like a young sword swallower practicing for my debut. I lowered Barbie's feet and legs into my mouth and then began sucking on them. They smelled like Jennifer and dirt and plastic. I sucked on her stubs and she told me it felt nice.

"You're better than a hot soak," Barbie said. I left her resting on my pillow and went downstairs to get us each a drink.

We were lying on my bed, curled into and out of each other. Barbie was on a pillow next to me and I was on my side facing her. She was talking about men, and as she talked I tried to be everything she said. She was saying she didn't like men who were afraid of themselves. I tried to be brave, to look courageous and secure. I held my head a certain way and it seemed to work. She said she didn't like men who were afraid of femininity, and I got confused.

"Guys always have to prove how boy they really are," Barbie said.

I thought of Jennifer trying to be a girl, wearing dresses,

doing her nails, putting makeup on, wearing a bra even though she wouldn't need one for about fifty years.

"You make fun of Ken because he lets himself be everything he is. He doesn't hide anything."

"He doesn't have anything to hide," I said. "He has tan molded plastic hair, and a bump for a dick."

"I never should have told you about the bump."

I lay back on the bed. Barbie rolled over, off the pillow, and rested on my chest. Her body stretched from my nipple to my belly button. Her hands pressed against me, tickling me.

"Barbie," I said.

"Umm Humm."

"How do you feel about me?"

She didn't say anything for a minute. "Don't worry about it," she said, and slipped her hand into my shirt through the space between the buttons.

Her fingers were like the ends of toothpicks performing some subtle ancient torture, a dance of boy death across my chest. Barbie crawled all over me like an insect who'd run into one too many cans of Raid.

Underneath my clothes, under my skin, I was going crazy. First off, I'd been kidnapped by my underwear with no way to manually adjust without attracting unnecessary attention.

With Barbie caught in my shirt I slowly rolled over, like in some space shuttle docking maneuver. I rolled onto my stomach, trapping her under me. As slowly and unobtrusively as possible, I ground myself against the bed, at first hoping it would fix things and then again and again, caught by a pleasure/pain principle.

"Is this a water bed?" Barbie asked.

My hand was on her breasts, only it wasn't really my hand, but more like my index finger. I touched Barbie and she made a little gasp, a squeak in reverse. She squeaked backwards, then stopped, and I was stuck there with my hand on her, thinking about how I was forever crossing a line between the haves and the have-nots, between good guys and bad, between men and animals, and there was absolutely nothing I could do to stop myself.

Barbie was sitting on my crotch, her legs flipped back behind her in a position that wasn't human.

At a certain point I had to free myself. If my dick was blue, it was only because it had suffocated. I did the honors and Richard popped out like an escape from maximum security.

"I've never seen anything so big," Barbie said. It was the sentence I dreamed of, but given the people Barbie normally hung out with, namely the bump boy himself, it didn't come as a big surprise.

She stood at the base of my dick, her bare feet buried in my pubic hair. I was almost as tall as she was. Okay, not almost as tall, but clearly we could be related. She and Richard even had the same vaguely surprised look on their faces.

She was on me and I couldn't help wanting to get inside her. I turned Barbie over and was on top of her, not caring if I killed her. Her hands pressed so hard into my stomach that it felt like she was performing an appendectomy.

I was on top, trying to get between her legs, almost breaking her in half. But there was nothing there, nothing to fuck except a small thin line that was supposed to be her ass crack.

I rubbed the thin line, the back of her legs and the space between her legs. I turned Barbie's back to me so I could do it without having to look at her face.

Very quickly, I came. I came all over Barbie, all over her and a little bit in her hair. I came on Barbie and it was the most horrifying experience I ever had. It didn't stay on her. It doesn't stick to plastic. I was finished. I was holding a come-covered Barbie in my hand like I didn't know where she came from.

Barbie said, "Don't stop," or maybe I just think she said that because I read it somewhere. I don't know anymore. I couldn't listen to her. I couldn't even look at her. I wiped myself off with a sock, pulled my clothes on, and then took Barbie into the bathroom.

At dinner I noticed Jennifer chewing her cuticles between bites of tuna-noodle casserole. I asked her if she was teething. She coughed and then started choking to death on either a little piece of fingernail, a crushed potato chip from the casserole, or maybe even a little bit of Barbie footie that'd stuck in her teeth. My mother asked her if she was okay.

"I swallowed something sharp," she said between coughs that were clearly influenced by the acting class she'd taken over the summer.

"Do you have a problem?" I asked her.

"Leave your sister alone," my mother said.

"If there are any questions to ask we'll do the asking," my father said.

"Is everything all right?" my mother asked Jennifer. She nodded. "I think you could use some new jeans," my mother said. "You don't seem to have many play clothes anymore."

"Not to change the subject," I said, trying to think of a way to stop Jennifer from eating Barbie alive.

"I don't wear pants," Jennifer said. "Boys wear pants."

"Your grandma wears pants," my father said.

"She's not a girl."

My father chuckled. He actually fucking chuckled. He's the only person I ever met who could actually fucking chuckle.

"Don't tell her that," he said, chuckling.

"It's not funny," I said.

"Grandma's are pull-ons anyway," Jennifer said. "They don't have a fly. You have to have a penis to have a fly."

"Jennifer," my mother said. "That's enough of that."

I decided to buy Barbie a present. I was at that strange point where I would have done anything for her. I took two buses and walked more than a mile to get to Toys R Us.

Barbie row was aisle 14C. I was a wreck. I imagined a million Barbies and having to have them all. I pictured fucking one, discarding it, immediately grabbing a fresh one, doing it, and then throwing it onto a growing pile in the corner of my room. An unending chore. I saw myself becoming a slave to Barbie. I wondered how many Tropical Barbies were made each year. I felt faint.

There were rows and rows of Kens, Barbies, and Skippers. Funtime Barbie, Jewel Secrets Ken, Barbie Rocker with "Hot Rockin' Fun and Real Dancin' Action." I noticed Magic Moves Barbie, and found myself looking at her carefully, flirtatiously, wondering if her legs were spreadable. "Push the switch and she moves," her box said. She winked at me while I was reading.

The only Tropical I saw was a black Tropical Ken. From just looking at him you wouldn't have known he was black. I mean, he wasn't black like anyone would be black. Black Tropical Ken was the color of a raisin, a raisin all spread out and unwrinkled. He had a short afro that looked like a wig had been dropped down and fixed on his head, a protective helmet. I wondered if black Ken was really white Ken sprayed over with a thick coating of ironed raisin plastic.

I spread eight black Kens out in a line across the front of a row. Through the plastic window of his box he told me he was hoping to go to dental school. All eight black Kens talked at once. Luckily, they all said the same thing at the same time. They said he really liked teeth. Black Ken smiled. He had the same white Pearl Drops, Pepsodent, Osmond family teeth that Barbie and white Ken had. I thought the entire Mattel family must take really good care of themselves. I figured they might be the only people left in America who actually brushed after every meal and then again before going to sleep.

I didn't know what to get Barbie. Black Ken said I should go for clothing, maybe a fur coat. I wanted something really special. I imagined a wonderful present that would draw us somehow closer.

There was a tropical pool and patio set, but I decided it might make her homesick. There was a complete winter holiday, with an A-frame house, fireplace, snowmobile, and sled. I imagined her inviting Ken away for a weekend without me. The six o'clock news set was nice, but because of her squeak, Barbie's future as an anchorwoman seemed limited. A workout center, a sofa bed and coffee table, a bubbling spa, a bedroom play set. I settled on the grand piano. It was $13.00. I'd always made it a point to never spend more than ten dollars on anyone. This time I figured, what the hell, you don't buy a grand piano every day.

"Wrap it up, would ya," I said at the checkout desk.

From my bedroom window I could see Jennifer in the backyard, wearing her tutu and leaping all over the place. It was dangerous as hell to sneak in and get Barbie, but I couldn't keep a grand piano in my closet without telling someone.

"You must really like me," Barbie said when she finally had the piano unwrapped.

I nodded. She was wearing a ski suit and skis. It was the

end of August and eighty degrees out. Immediately, she sat down and played "Chopsticks."

I looked out at Jennifer. She was running down the length of the deck, jumping onto the railing and then leaping off, posing like one of those red flying horses you see on old Mobil gas signs. I watched her do it once and then the second time, her foot caught on the railing, and she went over the edge the hard way. A minute later she came around the edge of the house, limping, her tutu dented and dirty, pink tights ripped at both knees. I grabbed Barbie from the piano bench and raced her into Jennifer's room.

"I was just getting warmed up," she said. "I can play better than that, really."

I could hear Jennifer crying as she walked up the stairs.

"Jennifer's coming," I said. I put her down on the dresser and realized Ken was missing.

"Where's Ken?" I asked quickly.

"Out with Jennifer," Barbie said.

I met Jennifer at her door. "Are you okay?" I asked. She cried harder. "I saw you fall."

"Why didn't you stop me?" she said.

"From falling?"

She nodded and showed me her knees.

"Once you start to fall no one can stop you." I noticed Ken was tucked into the waistband of her tutu.

"They catch you," Jennifer said.

I started to tell her it was dangerous to go leaping around with a Ken stuck in your waistband, but you don't tell someone who's already crying that they did something bad.

I walked her into the bathroom, and took out the hydrogen peroxide. I was a first aid expert. I was the kind of guy who walked around, waiting for someone to have a heart attack just so I could practice my CPR technique.

"Sit down," I said.

Jennifer sat down on the toilet without putting the lid down. Ken was stabbing her all over the place and instead of pulling him out, she squirmed around trying to get comfortable like she didn't know what else to do. I took him out for her. She watched as though I was performing surgery or something.

"He's mine," she said.

"Take off your tights," I said.

"No," she said.

"They're ruined," I said. "Take them off."

Jennifer took off her ballet slippers and peeled off her tights. She was wearing my old Underoos with superheroes on them, Spiderman and Superman and Batman all poking out from under a dirty dented tutu. I decided not to say anything, but it looked funny as hell to see a flat crotch in boys' underwear. I had the feeling they didn't bother making underwear for Ken because they knew it looked too weird on him.

I poured peroxide onto her bloody knees. Jennifer screamed into my ear. She bent down and examined herself, poking her purple fingers into the torn skin; her tutu bunched up and rubbed against her face, scraping it. I worked on her knees, removing little pebbles and pieces of grass from the area.

She started crying again.

"You're okay," I said. "You're not dying." She didn't care. "Do you want anything?" I asked, trying to be nice.

"Barbie," she said.

It was the first time I'd handled Barbie in public. I picked her up like she was a complete stranger and handed her to Jennifer, who grabbed her by the hair. I started to tell her to ease up, but couldn't. Barbie looked at me and I shrugged. I went downstairs and made Jennifer one of my special Diet Cokes.

"Drink this," I said, handing it to her. She took four giant gulps and immediately I felt guilty about having used a whole Valium.

"Why don't you give a little to your Barbie," I said. "I'm sure she's thirsty too."

Barbie winked at me and I could have killed her, first off for doing it in front of Jennifer, and second because she didn't know what the hell she was winking about.

I went into my room and put the piano away. I figured as long as I kept it in the original box I'd be safe. If anyone found it, I'd say it was a present for Jennifer.

Wednesday Ken and Barbie had their heads switched. I went to get Barbie, and there on top of the dresser were Barbie and Ken, sort of. Barbie's head was on Ken's body and Ken's head was on Barbie. At first I thought it was just me.

"Hi," Barbie's head said.

I couldn't respond. She was on Ken's body and I was looking at Ken in a whole new way.

I picked up the Barbie head/Ken and immediately Barbie's head rolled off. It rolled across the dresser, across the white doily past Jennifer's collection of miniature ceramic cats, and *boom* it fell to the floor. I saw Barbie's head rolling and about to fall, and then falling, but there was nothing I could do to stop it. I was frozen, paralyzed with Ken's headless body in my left hand.

Barbie's head was on the floor, her hair spread out underneath it like angel wings in the snow, and I expected to see blood, a wide rich pool of blood, or at least a little bit coming out of her ear, her nose, or her mouth. I looked at her head on the floor and saw nothing but Barbie with eyes like the cosmos looking up at me. I thought she was dead.

"Christ, that hurt," she said. "And I already had a head-ache from these earrings."

There were little red dot/ball earrings jutting out of Barbie's ears.

"They go right through my head, you know. I guess it takes getting used to," Barbie said.

I noticed my mother's pin cushion on the dresser next to the other Barbie/Ken, the Barbie body, Ken head. The pin cushion was filled with hundreds of pins, pins with flat silver ends and pins with red, yellow, and blue dot/ball ends.

"You have pins in your head," I said to the Barbie head on the floor.

"Is that supposed to be a compliment?"

I was starting to hate her. I was being perfectly clear and she didn't understand me.

I looked at Ken. He was in my left hand, my fist wrapped around his waist. I looked at him and realized my thumb was on his bump. My thumb was pressed against Ken's crotch and as soon as I noticed I got an auto-matic hard-on, the kind you don't know you're getting, it's just there. I started rubbing Ken's bump and watching my thumb like it was a large-screen projection of a porno movie.

"What are you doing?" Barbie's head said. "Get me up. Help me." I was rubbing Ken's bump/hump with my fin-ger inside his bathing suit. I was standing in the middle of my sister's room, with my pants pulled down.

"Aren't you going to help me?" Barbie kept asking. "Aren't you going to help me?"

In the second before I came, I held Ken's head hole in front of me. I held Ken upside down above my dick and came inside of Ken like I never could in Barbie.

I came into Ken's body and as soon as I was done I

wanted to do it again. I wanted to fill Ken and put his head back on, like a perfume bottle. I wanted Ken to be the vessel for my secret supply. I came in Ken and then I remembered he wasn't mine. He didn't belong to me. I took him into the bathroom and soaked him in warm water and Ivory liquid. I brushed his insides with Jennifer's toothbrush and left him alone in a cold-water rinse.

"Aren't you going to help me, aren't you?" Barbie kept asking.

I started thinking she'd been brain damaged by the accident. I picked her head up from the floor.

"What took you so long?" she asked.

"I had to take care of Ken."

"Is he okay?"

"He'll be fine. He's soaking in the bathroom." I held Barbie's head in my hand.

"What are you going to do?"

"What do you mean?" I said.

Did my little incident, my moment with Ken, mean that right then and there some decision about my future life as queerbait had to be made?"

"This afternoon. Where are we going? What are we doing? I miss you when I don't see you," Barbie said.

"You see me every day," I said.

"I don't really see you. I sit on top of the dresser and if you pass by, I see you. Take me to your room."

"I have to bring Ken's body back."

I went into the bathroom, rinsed out Ken, blew him dry with my mother's blow dryer, then played with him again. It was a boy thing, we were boys together. I thought sometime I might play ball with him, I might take him out instead of Barbie.

"Everything takes you so long," Barbie said when I got back into the room.

I put Ken back up on the dresser, picked up Barbie's body, knocked Ken's head off, and smashed Barbie's head back down on her own damn neck.

"I don't want to fight with you," Barbie said as I carried her into my room. "We don't have enough time together to fight. Fuck me," she said.

I didn't feel like it. I was thinking about fucking Ken and Ken being a boy. I was thinking about Barbie and Barbie being a girl. I was thinking about Jennifer, switching Barbie and Ken's heads, chewing Barbie's feet off, hanging Barbie from the ceiling fan, and who knows what else.

"Fuck me," Barbie said again.

I ripped Barbie's clothing off. Between Barbie's legs Jennifer had drawn pubic hair in reverse. She'd drawn it upside down so it looked like a fountain spewing up and out in great wide arcs. I spit directly onto Barbie and with my thumb and first finger rubbed the ink lines, erasing them. Barbie moaned.

"Why do you let her do this to you?"

"Jennifer owns me," Barbie moaned.

Jennifer owns me, she said, so easily and with pleasure. I was totally jealous. Jennifer owned Barbie and it made me crazy. Obviously it was one of those relationships that could only exist between women. Jennifer could own her because it didn't matter that Jennifer owned her. Jennifer didn't want Barbie, she had her.

"You're perfect," I said.

"I'm getting fat," Barbie said.

Barbie was crawling all over me, and I wondered if Jennifer knew she was a nymphomaniac. I wondered if Jennifer knew what a nymphomaniac was.

"You don't belong with little girls," I said.

Barbie ignored me.

There were scratches on Barbie's chest and stomach. She didn't say anything about them and so at first I pretended not to notice. As I was touching her, I could feel they were deep, like slices. The edges were rough; my finger caught on them and I couldn't help but wonder.

"Jennifer?" I said, massaging the cuts with my tongue, as though my tongue, like sandpaper, would erase them. Barbie nodded.

In fact, I thought of using sandpaper, but didn't know how I would explain it to Barbie: *you have to lie still and let me rub it really hard with this stuff that's like terrycloth dipped in cement.* I thought she might even like it if I made it into an S&M kind of thing and handcuffed her first.

I ran my tongue back and forth over the slivers, back and forth over the words "copyright 1966 Mattel Inc., Malaysia" tattooed on her back. Tonguing the tattoo drove Barbie crazy. She said it had something to do with scar tissue being extremely sensitive.

Barbie pushed herself hard against me, I could feel her slices rubbing my skin. I was thinking that Jennifer might kill Barbie. Without meaning to she might just go over the line and I wondered if Barbie would know what was happening or if she'd try to stop her.

We fucked, that's what I called it, fucking. In the beginning Barbie said she hated the word, which made me like it even more. She hated it because it was so strong and hard, and she said we weren't fucking, we were making love. I told her she had to be kidding.

"Fuck me," she said that afternoon and I knew the end was coming soon. "Fuck me," she said. I didn't like the sound of the word.

—

Friday when I went into Jennifer's room, there was something in the air. The place smelled like a science lab, a fire, a failed experiment.

Barbie was wearing a strapless yellow evening dress. Her hair was wrapped into a high bun, more like a wedding cake than something Betty Crocker would whip up. There seemed to be layers and layers of angel's hair spinning in a circle above her head. She had yellow pins through her ears and gold fuck-me shoes that matched the belt around her waist. For a second I thought of the belt and imagined tying her up, but more than restraining her arms or legs, I thought of wrapping the belt around her face, tying it across her mouth.

I looked at Barbie and saw something dark and thick like a scar rising up and over the edge of her dress. I grabbed her and pulled the front of the dress down.

"Hey big boy," Barbie said. "Don't I even get a hello?"

Barbie's breasts had been sawed at with a knife. There were a hundred marks from a blade that might have had five rows of teeth like shark jaws. And as if that wasn't enough, she'd been dissolved by fire, blue and yellow flames had been pressed against her and held there until she melted and eventually became the fire that burned herself. All of it had been somehow stirred with the lead of a pencil, the point of a pen, and left to cool. Molten Barbie flesh had been left to harden, black and pink plastic swirled together, in the crater Jennifer had dug out of her breasts.

I examined her in detail like a scientist, a pathologist, a fucking medical examiner. I studied the burns, the gouged-out area, as if by looking closely I'd find something, an explanation, a way out.

A disgusting taste came up into my mouth, like I'd been sucking on batteries. It came up, then sank back down into my stomach, leaving my mouth puckered with the bitter metallic flavor of sour saliva. I coughed and spit onto my shirt sleeve, then rolled the sleeve over to cover the wet spot.

With my index finger I touched the edge of the burn as lightly as I could. The round rim of her scar broke off under my finger. I almost dropped her.

"It's just a reduction," Barbie said. "Jennifer and I are even now."

Barbie was smiling. She had the same expression on her face as when I first saw her and fell in love. She had the same expression she always had and I couldn't stand it. She was smiling, and she was burned. She was smiling, and she was ruined. I pulled her dress back up, above the scar-line. I put her down carefully on the doily on top of the dresser and started to walk away.

"Hey," Barbie said, "aren't we going to play?"

About the Author

A. M. Homes was born in Washington, D.C., and attended Sarah Lawrence College and the University of Iowa Writers Workshop. In addition to *The Safety of Objects*, she is the author of the novel *Jack*.